HIDDEN SECRETS

Winx Club™

HIDDEN SECRETS

Adapted by Michael Anthony Steele

SCHOLASTIC INC.

New York   Toronto   London   Auckland   Sydney
Mexico City   New Delhi   Hong Kong   Buenos Aires

If you purchased this book without a cover, you should be aware that this book is stolen property. It was reported as "unsold and destroyed" to the publisher, and neither the author nor the publisher has received any payment for this "stripped book."

No part of this publication may be reproduced in whole or in part, or stored in a retrieval system, or transmitted in any form or by any means, electronic, mechanical, photocopying, recording, or otherwise, without the written permission of the publisher. For information regarding permission, write to Scholastic Inc., Attention: Permissions Department, 557 Broadway, New York, New York 10012.

Winx Club™ © 2005 Rainbow Srl. All rights reserved.

Published by Scholastic Inc. SCHOLASTIC and associated logos are trademarks and/or registered trademarks of Scholastic Inc.

ISBN 0-439-74424-5

12 11 10 9 8 7 6 5 4 3 2 1   5 6 7 8 9/0

Printed in the U.S.A.

First printing, July 2005

Winx Club™

CLUB

HIDDEN
SECRETS

CHAPTER 1

Bright sunlight poured in through the window and washed over Bloom's face. The warmth on her skin slowly lured her from her deep sleep. Her eyelids parted only to slam shut, blocking the brilliant light. The young girl rose and propped herself up on one elbow. She slowly rubbed her eyes with her free hand. Squinting, she let her eyes get accustomed to the sunlight — the very *bright* sunlight.

Too bright!

What time is it? Her eyes sprung wide-open. She must have overslept!

Bloom swung her legs off the bed. "Why didn't Flora wake me?" Bloom asked herself as she stumbled out of the tangle of sheets. "Professor Wizgiz is going to kill me for being late again!"

Bloom stopped and looked around her bedroom — *her* bedroom. Not the one she shared with Flora at the Alfea School for Fairies. She was in her own bedroom, back in her hometown of Gardenia. She had totally forgotten she was home for spring break.

She looked down and saw Kiko sitting up in his bed. The gray-and-white rabbit's ears stood straight up and his head cocked to one side. He flicked his whiskers and stared back at Bloom with a puzzled expression.

Bloom laughed and picked him up. "Sorry to scare you, Kiko," she said, giving him a hug. "I guess part of me is still back at school." The soft rabbit nuzzled her chin before she placed him back in his bed.

There was a knock on her door. "Bloom?" her mother said. "Are you up?"

"Yes, Mom," Bloom replied. "I'll be down in a minute."

Bloom showered, dressed, and then dried her long red hair. She supposed she could have used her magic to do the job instead of her hair dryer. However, she wasn't the expert on magical beauty secrets. That was her friend Stella. Bloom thought she'd better stick to the old-fashioned way for now. After all, she wouldn't want to end up bald her first day back in Gardenia.

With Kiko close behind, Bloom bounded down the stairs. She found her mother hard at work in the kitchen. Small stains covered her mother's blue apron. She blew a loose strand of her short brown hair away from her eyes. A smile stretched across her mother's face when Bloom entered the room.

"Something smells good," Bloom remarked. "Is that lunch?"

"Try supper," her mom said with a chuckle. She began chopping a carrot. "You missed lunch an hour ago."

Bloom put a hand to her stomach. "Maybe that's why I'm so hungry." She snatched up two carrot slices. She popped one into her mouth and handed the other to Kiko.

Bloom's mother handed her the knife and what was left of the carrot. "Why don't you give me a hand? I'm trying to get a head start on dinner before returning to the flower shop."

"Okay," Bloom replied. She chopped a few more slices off the carrot and popped another one into her mouth.

Bloom's mother pulled out another knife and began slicing an onion. "Bloom, honey," she said, "I want to talk to you about something that's been on my mind for awhile."

"Okay," said Bloom. "Go ahead."

"It's about when we adopted you," her mother continued.

"I know it was the greatest day of your life," Bloom chuckled.

"Well, of course it was the greatest day of my life," replied her mom. "You were such a cute, beautiful baby and you grew up so fast."

Bloom looked at her mother and smiled. She saw tears form in her mother's eyes. Was her mother upset? Then again, she *was* slicing onions.

"Honey, what I wanted to talk to you about . . ." her mom continued.

Bloom didn't hear anything else she said. Her attention was focused on a strange odor. "Hey, Mom, I think something's burning."

Her mother's eyes widened. "The roast!"

They turned to see black smoke billowing out of the oven. Bloom's mother reached for the door handle, but flames burst through the top of the door.

"Stand back, Mom!" ordered Bloom. "I'll get it!"

As Bloom concentrated on the oven, the door popped open, revealing a raging fire inside. Bloom raised a hand. "*Flame-us, extinguishus!*" she cried.

The fire dissolved to black smoke that Bloom drew out of the oven with a twirl of her finger. The smoke wound into a circle above her head.

"Honey?" Bloom's mom asked in a worried tone.

"Mom, I have to concentrate!" Bloom replied. "Don't worry, I know what I'm doing!" She raised both hands into the air. "*Aerolux!*" The swirling mass vanished in a small shower of golden sparkles.

Bloom's mother plopped into a nearby chair. She put a hand to her forehead and fanned her face with a dish-cloth.

Bloom placed a hand on her mother's shoulder. "Are you okay?"

Her mom looked up and smiled. "That was amazing!"

Bloom bit her lower lip. "I couldn't save the pot roast, though."

Her mother stood and gave Bloom a hug. "Never mind the pot roast," she said. "You saved us!"

CHAPTER 2

After her mother left for work, Bloom decided to ride her bike around Gardenia. As she pedaled the narrow streets of her hometown, Bloom remembered how she was disappointed when her parents first gave her the bike. She had been hoping they would buy her a scooter instead. Now, after all she'd been through, and what she'd discovered about the world, that feeling of disappointment seemed petty. In fact, it felt good to ride her bike and pretend she was just a normal girl again. For the moment, she didn't have to think of spells, fairies, or witches. She held out both arms, pretending she was flying — just like a normal girl would.

"Keep both hands on the handlebars, young lady!" said an authoritative voice beside her.

Bloom turned to see her father driving alongside her in a big red fire truck. "Hey, Dad!"

Her father slowed the truck to keep pace with Bloom's

bike. He removed his helmet and leaned out the window. His blond hair ruffled in the wind. "Did you sleep until noon again?" he asked with a grin.

"Maybe," replied Bloom with a smile of her own.

"I'm glad you're enjoying your first day of spring break. I want you to tell me all about it tonight," he said. "Now I've got to get back to the station," he said. "See you later!"

"Okay," Bloom said. "Have a good day, Dad!" She waved as he pulled ahead and continued down the street.

Bloom pedaled faster, as if trying to keep up with him. Then, as her dad's fire engine turned right, she zipped straight ahead. She was having a great time. No homework, no lab classes and, best of all, no witches to worry about. Before she went to Alfea, all she could do was think about fairies and magic. Now those things were the furthest from her mind.

As Bloom turned a corner, her tranquillity was abruptly interrupted. She saw something so odd that it had to be connected to the world of magic. She hit the brakes and brought her bike to a stop.

Ahead, near a small cluster of shops, many people were walking along the busy sidewalk. That wouldn't have been so strange in Gardenia or anywhere else. What *was* strange was the thing hovering above a young man. A long, smoky tendril snaked out of the man's back. Connected to the tendril was a purple cloud in a shape that resembled the man himself. The strange spirit energy seemed to have a mind of its own as well. As the man passed a bakery, the purple cloud hovered above a rack of pies. It seemed to enjoy their sweet aroma before hurrying to catch up with its owner.

At first, Bloom thought she might be seeing things. But then she saw another spirit attached to a woman crossing the street in front of her. This one turned and made eye contact.

"Hey, didn't you get the memo, Red?" asked the smoky spirit. "It's rude to stare!"

"Sorry," said Bloom.

The spirit turned up its smoky nose as it followed the woman across the street and out of sight.

Bloom began pedaling again and continued down the street. Along the way, she noticed several more wispy spirits attached to pedestrians. She supposed her Winx had grown stronger while she was at Alfea. Maybe these apparitions were there all along and now she was finally able to see them.

Bloom turned one last corner and headed for her mother's flower shop. As she got closer, she noticed a large black limousine parked out front. A man wearing a black cap sat in the driver's seat. He watched Bloom as she chained up her bike and entered the store.

Once inside, Bloom saw two men talking to her mother.

"Well, I am very excited about this," said her mom. "Why don't you just bring back the last form and . . ." Her mother noticed Bloom and waved her over. "Bloom, I'd like you to meet some people!" She put an arm around her daughter and gestured to the two men. "This is Mr. Bonner and Mr. Bonner."

"Hello!" said both men in unison. "How do you do?"

One of the Bonners was older with gray hair. The other one was taller, younger, and thinner. They resembled each other so much that they were clearly the Bonner brothers.

"Uh . . . hi," Bloom replied.

Bloom's mother was beaming. "These are my future business partners," she announced.

"Business partners?" asked Bloom.

"Your mother has agreed to sell her flower shop to us," said the older Bonner brother. He smiled a thin-lipped smile.

"Not entirely," her mother corrected. "They'll own the actual shop, but I'll still own the shop name. See, they think . . ."

"That we can turn this shop into a big chain of stores," the thinner Bonner brother interrupted.

Bloom let out a small gasp as she looked over their heads. A dark cloud floated over each brother. Each dark mass resembled the man below it. Then the spirits spoke.

"It's amazing how foolish people are when you promise them the world," said the spirit belonging to the younger Bonner.

"We're going to make a bundle on this shop!" the other spirit agreed.

"Like I always say," the younger spirit said with a chuckle, "people are just like lollipops — underneath they're all suckers."

The Bonners didn't seem to notice how Bloom stared a few inches over their heads. Bloom's mother didn't notice, either. She continued her conversation with the two men. "Bring that last form right back and we'll be all set," she said.

"Sure thing!" said the brothers, once more in unison.

The two men nodded politely, then left the shop. Bloom's mother waved and then turned toward Bloom. "Pretty exciting, isn't it?" she asked. She practically bubbled over with excitement. "Your mother is going to be a joint owner of a company!"

Bloom was stunned and didn't answer. Instead, she watched as the large black limo pulled into the street and out of sight.

"Bloom?" asked her mother.

"Uh . . ." Bloom began and then glanced around the room. She couldn't tell her mother what she had seen, could she? Who would believe such a strange thing? Then again, being at Alfea, she'd seen odder things in the past few weeks. Her mother hadn't though. How would she react?

Bloom quickly spotted a box of plastic flowers on the floor. "Do these go on the shelf?"

"Yes, but . . ."

"Cool!" said Bloom as she grabbed the box and placed it on an empty shelf behind the counter.

"Honey, is everything all right?" her mother asked.

"Everything's great," Bloom replied, quickly looking around for something else to put away. "Why wouldn't it be?"

"Well, for one thing," her mother said, "you haven't congratulated me. This partnership could be a very exciting opportunity for me. If the shop starts franchising . . ."

Bloom couldn't keep quiet any longer. "Mom, these guys are taking advantage of you!"

"Taking advantage of me?" her mom asked. "What do you mean?"

"Well, I'm not exactly sure, but . . ." Bloom began, trying to think of a way to explain what she had seen.

"But what, Bloom?" her mom pressed.

Bloom sighed and just said it. "I think I can see people's inner spirits."

Her mother wrinkled her brow. "Okay," she said, "and what does that mean?"

"I guess that means I can see their true nature or something," Bloom explained.

"Is this something they taught you at Alfea?" inquired her mom.

"No, it isn't," Bloom replied. "And it's never happened to me until today."

"So then, how do you know?"

"Mom, I just know it." Bloom hoped her mother would just trust her on this. "These guys are trying to trick you. They're trying to steal your store!"

CHAPTER 3

Bloom hung around the shop until the Bonner brothers returned with the rest of the paperwork. When they entered the shop, she didn't see the strange apparitions hovering over their heads. Then again, she didn't have to. Once her mother told them the news, their true nature showed itself.

"I don't understand why you've changed your mind," said the young Bonner brother. His face began to flush red.

"Yes, why'd you change your mind?" asked the older Bonner. "We had a deal."

"We had a deal," the younger Bonner repeated in a louder tone. He pointed to the stack of legal papers on the counter. "You said to bring the last form right back. Did something happen?"

The brothers scowled with anger, but Bloom's mother maintained a cheery expression. "No, nothing happened," she replied. "I just realized I was getting in over my head. I like things the way they are — simple."

"This couldn't be simpler," said the younger Bonner, forcing a smile. "You've already signed most of the forms. All you have to do is sign the last one."

"No, thank you," said her mom. "I like my business the way it is and I'm afraid I'm going to have to keep it that way."

The two men said nothing. Instead, the black spirits reappeared over them. The smoky versions of the men glowered and trembled with anger.

Finally, the older brother broke the silence. "Look, we want this shop!" Hatred flashed in his eyes. "And we have plenty of ways of getting what we want!"

Bloom's mother dropped her pleasant facade. "And what's that supposed to mean?"

The younger man's thin lips stretched to reveal a wicked grin. "Oh, nothing," he said casually. "It's just that there are other things that can be broken besides agreements."

With that said, the older brother pretended to yawn. In an exaggerated gesture, he stretched out his arms and swept a potted plant off the counter. It crashed on the floor, shattering its decorative porcelain pot.

"The Amonum Maximum!" cried Bloom's mom.

"How clumsy of me," snickered the older brother. The two apparitions bellowed loudly, but only Bloom could hear their laughter.

Bloom's mother now wore a scowl of her own. Yet she remained somewhat polite — too polite in Bloom's opinion. "I've said what I had to say, now please leave."

"We'll be back," warned the younger Bonner. "This will be our shop, one way or another!"

The two Bonners stormed out of the shop. Their wicked spirits trailed after them. After their limousine pulled away, Bloom's mother shook her head and looked down at the mess on the floor. "You were right about those men, Bloom."

Bloom extended a hand to the fallen plant. "Check out this trick my friend Flora taught me." Golden shafts of light erupted from her palm. They sprinkled over the wilting plant like a gentle summer rain. "Flora hates to see a plant with a broken home." In a flash of bright light, the plant and broken pot quickly vanished and reappeared whole again. It looked as it did before the Bonner brothers tampered with it.

"Whoa!" said Bloom's mom. She picked up the potted plant and set it back on the counter. "Come here, you!" She gave Bloom a big hug.

For the next few days, Bloom spent as much time with her parents as she could. They saw movies, strolled through the park, and went out to dinner. Even though she missed the friends she had made at Alfea, it felt good being with her family again. They had such a great time that the nasty incident with the Bonner brothers was quickly forgotten. Unfortunately, it would come crashing back all too soon.

When Bloom wasn't sleeping late, or riding her bike around Gardenia, she helped in her mother's flower shop.

One morning, as she swept the floor, a loud crash broke the peaceful tranquillity of the day.

"What in the world?" her mother asked.

They both ran to the front of the store where they found a brick lying amid shards of broken glass from the front door. Bloom picked up the brick as her mother ran outside.

"It's a good thing this didn't hit anybody," said Bloom. She joined her mother outside. "Do you see who threw it?"

Her mother scanned the area. It was early enough that only a few shoppers walked the sidewalks. "I don't see anyone suspicious." She turned her attention to the broken glass door. "Now I'll have to replace the door and that's not going to be cheap."

Bloom looked at the brick in her hand. "Not to worry," she said. Bloom concentrated on the brick. In a flash of light, the brick transformed into a large yellow eraser. Bloom held it up to the shattered glass. "*Damagus, erasus!*" The eraser glowed and Bloom waved it in front of the broken door. As she moved, the glass seemed to melt back into place. It was as if she erased away the break entirely.

"That's great!" her mother exclaimed. "Having a fairy for a daughter is quite handy!"

Her mother went back to work on an arrangement she had been preparing. She seemed without a care in the world. Bloom wasn't so carefree. She suspected the tossed brick had something to do with the Bonners.

Bloom swept up the shards of glass and dumped them

into the trashcan. She tried to throw away her suspicions with the broken debris. Maybe some kid threw the brick as a prank. After all, her mother had run outside right after it happened. A kid could have dashed down the sidewalk and ducked down some alley. She had trouble picturing one of the Bonner brothers in his black business suit, running away.

Either way, Bloom had done what she could. She decided not to dwell on it anymore. And for the rest of the morning, she didn't think of it at all. Instead, Bloom enjoyed building arrangements, transplanting flowers into decorative pots, and waiting on customers. She was with her mother and that's all that mattered.

CHAPTER 4

Bloom and her mother strolled through downtown Gardenia. They gazed in shopwindows as they navigated the lightly crowded sidewalks on the way back to the flower shop.

"That lunch was amazing!" said Bloom's mom.

Bloom put a hand to her stomach. "I know. I'm so stuffed."

As they turned the corner, Bloom's mother reached into her purse and removed a set of keys. The flower shop came into view. "Now, Bloom," she said, "your grandmother used to say that a lady is never stuffed, she's . . ." Her mother dropped her keys and put both hands to her mouth. "Oh no!"

"What's wrong, Mom?" asked Bloom.

Her mother dashed forward and pushed open the unlocked door to the shop. "The door's been forced open. Someone was here while we were gone!"

"What?" asked Bloom. She looked down and saw fresh scrapes around the lock on the door.

Her mother stepped into the shop. "Oh my! Look at this place!"

The entire store was in shambles. Vases were smashed, display cases were shattered, and shelves were toppled. Dirt, leaves, and flower petals littered the floor. All of the arrangements had been torn apart. It even looked as if someone had stripped several stems of all their leaves and buds. Nothing was left untouched.

"I don't suppose you have a spell for this," her mom said hopefully.

"No," Bloom answered. Maybe if she were a senior she'd know what to do. But for now, she could only repair much smaller objects. "I'm sorry, Mom."

Her mother stepped gingerly over the debris as she moved deeper into the store. "I don't get it," she said. "Why would burglars wreck the place? It just doesn't make any sense."

Bloom carefully followed. The incident with the brick by itself could have been just a kid. However, two acts of vandalism in the same day? There could be only one answer.

"I don't think it was a burglar," Bloom announced. She made her way to the main counter. "It was the two Mr. Bonners."

"Now, we don't know that, Bloom," said her mother.

"We can't just start pointing fingers." She sighed and scanned the room again. "There has been a problem with burglary lately. I saw it on the news."

Bloom opened the cash register and pulled out a wad of money. "If it was burglars, why didn't they take the money from the register?" she asked. "It was those guys. They're trying to intimidate you!"

Later that evening, Bloom helped her mother wash the dishes. Nobody had said much at dinner. The silence seemed worse now. Her mother dried plates and put them away while her father sat at the table nursing a cup of coffee.

"What did the police say again?" her dad asked for what seemed like the hundredth time.

"Same as before, Mike," her mother sighed. "They were there all afternoon, but they said there wasn't enough evidence."

"That really steams my coffee," he said through clenched teeth. "We can't just let these guys get away with it!"

"There's no point in getting all worked up," said her mother. "We'll figure something out."

Bloom's father began to take a sip then set the cup down on the table. "I know. I just worry about you." He picked up a spoon and stirred the coffee aimlessly. "I don't want anything bad to happen to you."

Bloom's mother put a plate away then glided over to her husband. She placed two gentle hands on his shoulders and rubbed. "I know," she said.

Her father sighed. "I guess we'll figure this out tomorrow.

I need to hit the pillows." He stood and ambled for the stairs. "Good-night, Bloom."

Bloom's mother followed. "Good-night, Bloom."

"Good-night, Mom. Good-night, Dad," Bloom replied.

As her parents went upstairs, Bloom lifted a plate from the soapy water. She held it in front of her and the suds slid down, revealing her reflection beyond. Bloom had all these powers now, yet she felt powerless to help her parents.

CHAPTER 5

Bloom had a difficult time falling asleep that night. She tossed and turned and couldn't shake the feeling that something terrible was going to happen. Worst of all, her mind raced trying to think of ways she could help her parents. Back at school, she had battled dreadful witches ten times more dangerous than two greedy businessmen. But here in Gardenia, she seemed powerless. It was as if she didn't belong anymore. Maybe she never belonged.

Bloom didn't find peace when she finally drifted to sleep. Instead, her head filled with nightmares. The last one had her standing in a room filled with flowers. They smelled sweet and were more beautiful than any she had ever seen. She reached out to take one, to bring it to her nose so she could inhale its scent and remember it forever. However, when she touched its stem, the lovely flower turned to ash. It disintegrated in her hand. She tried another and the same thing happened. Then another. And another. Soon, she didn't have to touch the flowers. They simply dissolved when she looked at them. Before long, the entire collection crumbled away around her. Mounds of ash surrounded her.

Then, as if time ran backward, the ash erupted into flames. She was surrounded by fire. Smoke filled the air and she could barely breath. The immense heat seemed to engulf her where she stood. She had to get out of there. She had to flee but she couldn't. Bloom was completely surrounded by roaring wildfire. The flames were so bright she held her eyes shut as tight as she could. But it did no good. The brilliant light shone through her closed eyelids. Then, in the distance, she swore she heard a baby crying.

"Aaaaaaaaaaaaah!!" Bloom screamed as she opened her eyes and sat up in bed. She was out of breath and covered in sweat. She coughed and gagged as if her lungs were really filled with smoke.

Her door swung open. "Bloom?" asked her father.

"Are you okay?" asked her mother.

"The flower shop!" she said between coughs. She threw off her blanket. "We have to go!"

"It's okay, honey," her father said as he sat beside her. He put a comforting hand on her shoulder. "You had a nightmare."

Bloom leapt to her feet and put on her shoes. "No, I had a vision!" she cried. "Mom's shop is on fire, we have to go now!"

Her father didn't argue. Instead, the three of them ran downstairs. With Bloom in her sweats, and her parents still in pajamas, they piled into the car and took off downtown.

"Hurry, Dad," Bloom pleaded.

An experienced firefighter, Bloom's father drove fast yet safely. He knew all the quickest routes through town and got them there in record time. But when they turned the final corner, Bloom saw that they were too late.

The car screeched to a halt in front of the flower shop. Flames erupted from broken windows as smoke billowed up to the sky.

"Quick, Mike, call your squad!" yelled Bloom's mom.

The three got out of the car and watched as the fire grew.

Bloom's father pulled the hand-mike from the car's radio. "Chimney Rock, it's Honey Bee," he said. "We've got a fire in progress at Third and Carroll. Get here ASAP!"

Her mother began to cry. "My shop! Mike!"

Bloom's dad wrapped his arms around her mom. "Don't worry, honey. It's going to be okay." He held her tightly as she buried her face in his shoulder. "At least you weren't in there," he added.

Bloom couldn't believe it. With all her power and Winx, she couldn't stop two bitter men from lighting a match and burning her mother's dreams to the ground. Anger welled inside her. The more her mother cried, the angrier Bloom became.

Her father still tried to console her mother. "We can always replace the shop. But we can't replace you."

Bloom wiped the tears from her own eyes and marched toward the burning building. "I'm taking care of this," she announced. "You guys stand back!"

"Bloom, no!" her mother yelled behind her. "Stop her, Mike!"

Bloom felt pressure on her arm as her dad grabbed her and held her back. "No, Bloom!" he said. "The boys are on their way."

Bloom spun to face him. "The station is on the other side of town, Dad." She pointed to what was left of the shop. "If we don't do something quick, the fire will spread. Let me at least try to contain it."

Her father shook his head. "Bloom, there's nothing you can do."

"Yes, there is!" she insisted. "I'll use my magic!"

Her father stared at her for a moment. Then he released his grip. "Okay, you can try," he said. "But you're taking me with you."

CHAPTER 6

Bloom's father walked close behind her as they moved deeper into the flower shop. Flames surrounded them on all sides and climbed the surrounding walls and shelves like blazing vines. Fortunately, neither Bloom nor her father felt any of their heat.

"So this force field thing totally protects us from the flames?" asked her dad.

"Yes," Bloom replied. She inched forward and the surrounding, golden force field moved with her. "But the spell will only last for ten minutes."

"Wow, pretty awesome!" Bloom's father looked around in amazement. "We have to get a couple of these things down at the station."

Bloom didn't hear him. Instead, her eyes were transfixed on the flames. Their hypnotic dancing carried her back to her dream. As before, the flowers around them turned to ash. And as before, she heard a baby's cry.

"Do you hear that?" she asked.

"Hear what?" asked her dad. "Bloom?"

Bloom was in another fire now. In an unknown building. Firemen battled the blaze but the flames were too strong. The building was old and going up fast. Most of the firemen were pulling out. All of them would retreat and battle the fire from outside. All of them but one.

"Come on, let's go!" yelled a retreating fireman. He grabbed the shoulder of a young, blond fireman. "The fire's too big, Mike! We have to get out of here!"

"I'm going in!" Mike shouted. He shook off the other man's hand and darted deeper into the burning building.

Bloom was there but she was not there. She saw the younger version of her father venture deeper into the burning building. Then she heard the crying baby again.

Her father must have heard it, too. "I'm coming," he yelled. "I'm going to save you!"

Bloom watched as her father's younger self turned a corner and saw the source of the cries. A tiny red-haired baby lay wrapped in a blanket beneath a golden force field. The sparkling dome was identical to the one they had just used to enter the flower shop.

"What the . . . ?" asked Bloom's younger father.

Another voice echoed through the flames — a woman's voice. "Save her. . . . Take care of her . . ."

"I don't believe this," said the young man. He reached through the force field and gently picked her up. "Don't be afraid, little girl." The tiny baby smiled at him. "You're in my arms now."

Bloom, the voice echoed. *Bloom*.

"Bloom?"

She was back in the flower shop.

"Bloom!" shouted her father. He pointed past her. "Look!"

Now completely out of her trance, Bloom saw where her dad was pointing. An older man in a dark suit cowered on the floor. She recognized him immediately. "That's the Bonners' driver!" she shouted.

"I'll get him," Mike announced. He stepped through the force field and extended a hand to the frightened man. "Stay calm, sir. We've got you."

Coughing, the man staggered to his feet and toward her father's hand. "Thank you," he said. Her father took off his coat and wrapped it around the weak man.

"Take the side exit!" Bloom instructed. "I can take care of everything in here." Bloom's father gave her a worried look. "Don't worry, Dad," she reassured him.

"Be careful," said her father. He helped the man to the side door.

Once they were safely out of the building, Bloom saw the force field flicker. Time was running out. She extended her arms and concentrated on the power inside her. Her hands began to glow as she willed the flames to extinguish. Slowly, a swirling mass of sparkling light danced before her. The magical whirlpool spun faster and the surrounding flames seemed drawn to it. Bloom closed her eyes and concentrated harder. This was the crucial moment. Just as she had extinguished the flames in her mother's kitchen, she would do the same here, but on a grander scale.

Bloom's hands grew warmer. It felt as if the flames were licking them as they were sucked through the vortex. She knew better. She had felt this sensation before. What she felt now was the fire *inside* her. It burned brightly, giving Bloom her power.

She opened her eyes just in time to see the last of the blaze disappear through the swirling portal. It, too, was vanishing, drawing in a last few tendrils of smoke as it went. All that was left were the charred remains of the shop and a few burning coals. Outside, wailing sirens approached.

"Good," said Bloom. "They're finally here."

CHAPTER
7

Firemen rolled up wet hoses and carried equipment back to their trucks. A wet, black sludge pile was all that remained of the flower shop. Luckily, no one was hurt. And the fire hadn't spread to the surrounding buildings.

The limo driver sat at the back of one of the fire engines. A blanket was wrapped around his shivering body. "I don't know what you were doing in there," he said, "but that sure was something."

"What were *you* doing in there?" asked Bloom.

The driver took a sip of water, then gave Bloom an embarrassed look. "I drove the Bonner brothers to the store," he said. "But when I saw them start the fire, I tried to stop them. That's when they knocked me out."

Bloom's mother looked at what was left of her flower shop. Tears formed in her eyes. "They caused all this trouble just because I wouldn't sell them my store?"

"They sure did," answered the driver. "They figured that this way you would *have* to sign the contract."

"Yeah, well, they were wrong," Bloom's dad said angrily. "Now they're in a lot of trouble. And you may be, too."

"I know," agreed the driver. "I shouldn't have had anything to do with them but I felt as if I had no choice." He took another sip of water. "You see, I used to own a limo business until they scammed me out of it. I only took this job because I needed the money. I have a family to support." The man shivered again and pulled the blanket over his shoulders. "But tonight, starting a fire, they went too far." He looked into Bloom's eyes. "I could never be a part of that!"

Bloom thought he was telling the truth.

"Believe me, I'm sorry," he added.

"I know," said Bloom. She saw a smoky apparition hovering over the driver. The wispy figure clutched his head in agony and guilt. "I can see that you are."

On the last day of her spring break, the mayor of Gardenia held a special ceremony for Bloom and her family. He was grateful for their help in bringing down the Bonner brothers. Apparently, Bloom's mother wasn't the only small business owner currently being bullied by the Bonners. Bloom also received special recognition for having the courage to save the limo driver.

After the ceremony, Bloom made peanut-butter-and-jelly sandwiches for lunch.

"As if it weren't enough to be town heroes," said her mother. "Between the money I'm getting from the insurance, and the reward from the mayor, I'll be able to open an even bigger flower shop than before!"

"As long as you install the best alarm system on the market," her father added, "it sounds great."

As her parents ate lunch, Bloom thought about what she had seen in the fire. Her father must have noticed her deep in thought. "Hey, Bloom, are you okay?" he asked. "It's not like you to let a peanut-butter-and-jelly sandwich go uneaten."

"Is there something bothering you, sweetie?" asked her mother.

"Yes, there is," Bloom replied. "During the fire, I had this sort of . . . vision." She looked up at her father. "I saw Dad in a fire with a newborn baby," said Bloom. "He was saving the baby."

Her parents exchanged worried glances. Then they looked down.

"What?" asked Bloom. "You know something about this?"

Her mother sighed. "Yes, we do." She paused a moment, seeming to gather courage. "This is what I was trying to tell you the other day."

"What?" asked Bloom. "What is it?"

Her father took over. "You see, honey, we talked to you about being adopted, but what we didn't talk about was that day in the fire, when I found you."

Bloom stood and leaned over the table. "What do you mean you found me in a fire? What was I doing there?"

"We don't know, Bloom," her dad replied. "I thought I heard a voice calling to me."

"A voice?" asked Bloom.

"I know it sounds strange." He scratched the back of his head. "You see . . . the fire was a big one, a four-alarmer. Three blocks were burning and there was no way to stop it." He smiled. "But when I picked you up, the whole fire went out. Just like that. You clearly had the most powerful and amazing magic."

Bloom felt her eyes fill with tears. "Why didn't you tell me about it before?" she asked. "Did you think that there was something weird or wrong with me, that I wasn't normal?"

"No, Bloom," her father reassured her. "Of course not."

"When you told me about being adopted, why didn't you tell me about this, too?" asked Bloom.

Her mother stood and put her arms around Bloom's shoulders. "We were going to," she said. "But since your magic never came back, we thought we'd wait till you were old enough to understand."

"Then there was that day you met Stella in the park," her dad added.

"And your powers came back stronger than ever," her mom explained. "You went right off to Alfea so quickly — before we could sit down and talk with you."

"Let me tell you something important, sweetie." Her mother squeezed her tightly. "We did talk to you about the real magic that happened that day." She slowly turned Bloom and wiped the tears from her eyes. "The magic was that we found you and you found us and that we became a family."

Her father stood and put his arms around both of them. "Bloom, sweetie, we love you so much."

Bloom hugged them tightly. "I love you guys, too."

CHAPTER 8

When Bloom returned to Alfea, her four closest friends gathered in her and Flora's room. They sat quietly on the bed while Bloom told them all about her spring break. When she finished, Bloom didn't feel as cheerful as the happy ending in her story. She sat there quietly as she stroked Kiko's soft fur.

"I don't get it," said Musa. She cocked her head sharply, flapping her two dark pigtails.

"Yeah, Bloom," said Flora. "Why are you down?" She placed her gentle hand on one of Bloom's. "If you ask me, that was a beautiful story." She brushed a strand of her long brown hair away from her face. "I think you and your parents have a terrific relationship."

"You talk about real things with them," added Tecna. She stood and crossed her arms. "That seems like a fine quality in a family dynamic."

"Girl, your Earth parents sound like awesome people," Musa added.

"That's just it," Bloom explained. "They're my *Earth* parents. You see?"

Stella got to her feet, as well. Her flowing blond hair swayed gracefully. "This new info has you curious about your birth parents, hasn't it?" asked Stella.

"Of course it does," said Bloom. "I'm probably not even from Earth."

"So then, what were you doing in a fire in Gardenia?" asked Tecna.

"That's what I'd like to know," Bloom replied. "Who put me there? Was my dad meant to find me? And what was that voice?"

Flora stroked Bloom's hair. "You may never find the answers. You know that, don't you?"

"Would that stop you from looking?" asked Bloom.

Flora smiled. "Probably not."

Bloom placed Kiko beside her and slid off the bed. "No matter what it takes, I want to find out. Where did I come from? What realm in what part of the universe?" She paced to the other side of the room. "I have to find out about my origins." She turned to her four best friends. "So, will you help me?"

Stella was the first to join her. "I know I'll help you, Bloom!" She gave a sly wink. "Sticking my nose in other people's business is my favorite pastime!"

Musa hopped up and joined them. "You can count me in!" She turned back to the bed. "Flora?"

"Of course," said Flora as she glided toward the group.

"Sign me up!" said Tecna, completing the circle of friends.

"After all," Musa said as she placed a hand in the center of the circle. "We're the Winx Club!"

"The Winx Club!" Stella echoed.

"The Winx Club!" said everyone in unison.

Bloom laughed and felt happy for the first time since her return from Gardenia. She had missed her parents a little and the new knowledge of her adoption had been bothering her. However, now she was back with her friends, her new family at Alfea. She knew that they would gladly help her on her quest. She knew she could count on them for anything.

CHAPTER
9

The following week, Bloom jumped right back into her classes. With so much homework, it seemed as if her professors didn't take a vacation like the students did. It was as if they had stayed at Alfea the entire week just thinking up new assignments, lab spells, and exams.

One particularly difficult exam was given by Headmistress Faragonda herself. Bloom was dreading it. She really liked Miss Faragonda. However, this exam was supposed to test her reaction time, dexterity, and skill under pressure. And since the test took place in the main gymnasium, in front of the entire student body, there would certainly be vast amounts of pressure.

Once everyone had filed into the gym, Miss Faragonda stood and addressed the students. "Your final exam is the laser beam obstacle course." The older woman's gray hair sat in its usual bun atop her head. She paused to inspect the students over the rims of her thin glasses. Then she gestured to the course below. "As usual, we'll go in alphabetical order," she said to the fairy-filled bleachers. "That means Bloom will go first."

Bloom stood, and shuffled past the neighboring seats and down the aisle. "I'm always first," she said to herself. "Maybe next time we could try reverse alphabetical order."

Bloom stepped out onto the empty arena floor. She extended the first two fingers on each hand, crossed her arms, and concentrated on turning into a fairy. Using her Winx, Bloom levitated off the ground. She closed her eyes and felt a magical fire ignite over her entire body. It burned away her old clothes and formed new ones. Fire engulfed her, creating long gloves on her arms, boots on her feet, and a sparkling, blue two-piece over her body. Bloom felt the familiar tug on her back as her set of fairy wings sprouted. Bloom opened her eyes and hovered above the ground, waiting for the headmistress's orders.

"Your goal," Miss Faragonda began, "is to get the floating rose to the pedestal."

Bloom looked up and noticed a floating crystal globe hovering high above the center of the gym. She then followed the headmistress's pointing finger to a short, gold pedestal located at the other end of the large building.

"If you get hit by three obstacles," Miss Faragonda continued, "you're out. Ready? Go!"

Bloom dropped to the ground as a blue beam of light shot over her head. She immediately had to roll to the left to dodge another one. It seemed as if blue laser beams were the obstacles for this test. They flickered on and off as they crisscrossed the entire gym floor.

Bloom was doing all right at first. However, it seemed as if every time she steered clear of one beam, three more would appear to take its place. She was having a tough time with the new test. Luckily, she could hear her friends cheering for her.

"Watch out, Bloom!" shouted Flora's distant voice.

"You can do it," yelled Musa.

With renewed confidence, Bloom performed a backflip and dodged three more laser beams. Unfortunately, she extended her leg too far and was struck in her ankle by one of the blue rays. It didn't hurt at all. She merely felt a tingling sensation on her skin.

"That's one," announced Miss Faragonda.

Bloom sprang forward to avoid another blue shaft of light. She landed in a crouch, then ducked as another beam shot over her head. As she looked for the next hazard, she felt her right hand tingle.

"That's two," said Miss Faragonda.

Bloom didn't know what was wrong. She should have been doing much better. Up until now, she had been busy dodging laser beams. She hadn't even attempted to grab the rose. She looked up at the floating orb. That was it! Since Bloom had spent so much time in Gardenia, she was still thinking like an Earth girl. She had been running, jumping, and dodging. She was a fairy. She could fly!

Bloom spread her wings and propelled herself upward. Laser beams lashed out at her, but she easily veered out of their way. With the tiniest flicks of her gossamer wings, she twirled and somersaulted in midair.

"Good one, Bloom!" Musa cheered.

Bloom dodged two more beams then flew straight for the rose. She snatched it up without even slowing down. She flew high to the gym ceiling, turned, and then folded her wings. Bloom dove rapidly, twirling and looping as the blue beams of light erupted around her. They seemed to be moving at a snail's pace now. She felt like nothing could touch her.

Bloom landed in front of the golden pedestal. She held the globe over it and looked toward the stands. She smiled when she saw her friends' supporting faces.

"Don't forget," warned Miss Faragonda, "other obstacles will be added along the way!"

Bloom saw her friends' faces change. They went from joy to concern in the blink of an eye. Their mouths dropped as they peered at something over Bloom's head. With her hands still holding the globe mere inches above the pedestal, Bloom looked up. A giant, blue energy ball had formed over her. Before she could do anything about it, the ball flew down and crashed into her.

CHAPTER 10

"**I was *that* close**," said Bloom. She listlessly pushed around the tiny scoop of ice cream in her bowl. "But I couldn't seem to summon my power."

Bloom propped up her head with her other hand. She sat across the table from Brandon. He was one of the boys from Red Fountain School of Heroics and Bravery. He was the cutest boy at Red Fountain as far as Bloom was concerned. She was very happy that he had invited her out for ice cream. Unfortunately, she didn't think she was very good company right now.

"Don't get so bummed out about it," said Brandon. "It's just a test."

"I know." She began to take a bite of ice cream, then returned the spoon to the bowl. "It's just that my power is so frustrating sometimes."

Brandon reached across the table and held her hand. "Come on, Bloom. Your power is awesome."

Bloom gave him a halfhearted smile. "The thing is, I

can't control it." She sighed. "And sometimes I can't connect to it at all."

"Maybe that's just because it's new," Brandon suggested.

"If I could just figure out where my power came from," said Bloom, "then I might be able to finally understand how it works."

"Good point," Brandon agreed. "You know, I could help you look."

"Thanks." Bloom's smile widened and she squeezed his hand. "But the only place I know to look is in the Book Chamber at Cloud Tower and that's way too dangerous."

A few weeks ago, Bloom and her friends had sneaked into the dreaded Cloud Tower School for Witches. While she was there, she had stumbled across a magical book written completely about her. She didn't get a chance to examine it thoroughly. But what she found made her definitely want to go back and read more.

Brandon smiled and looked deeply into her eyes. "Don't worry," he said. "We'll think of something."

CHAPTER
11

Mirta doodled in her notebook. It was one of the many diversions she used in order to stay awake in Headmistress Griffin's Spells class. The young freshman wasn't having the best time at Cloud Tower School. She had always thought being a powerful witch would be the coolest thing ever. However, when she arrived, she began to change her mind. Many of the other girls there were rude, crude, and just plain mean. Mirta vowed to stick it out though. She wasn't about to give up no matter how long Headmistress Griffin droned on and on about nasty spells.

"My personal favorite," said Miss Griffin, "is a revenge spell passed down from my grandmother." Her thin lips stretched into a wicked grin. "I won't tell you all of its secret ingredients. But I will tell you that it contains three different types of roadkill." Her eyes flashed with delight. "Now I want you to describe your favorite spells. You're first, Mirta."

Mirta was wide-awake now. She jumped at the mention of her name and clambered out of her seat. She timidly walked down the aisle to the head of the large classroom. She wished her heavy boots didn't make so much noise. The short, auburn-haired girl didn't like being the center of attention. However, she now felt the eyes of the other students on her.

"Okay," she said as she turned toward the rest of the class. "This one works best outdoors and it's most effective during a solar eclipse." She wrung her hands nervously. "You hold a gemstone above your head and say 'friends forever' four times." She looked over her shoulder at Miss Griffin. "The spell works quickly to bring you your very own best friend."

For a moment there was only silence. Then the entire class erupted in laughter. Miss Griffin raised a hand to silence them. Mirta's eyes widened as the headmistress glowered at her.

"Excuse me?" asked the headmistress. "Did you say the spell makes a friend?"

As Mirta nodded her head, she heard a few snickers behind her.

Miss Griffin snapped her fingers and a black quill appeared in her hand. "Mirta, you fail for the day. Sit down." She scribbled her failing grade into her roll book.

As Mirta shuffled back to her seat, she heard whispered insults from the other students. "What a dork," said one girl. "She's so pathetic," said another. She heard, "The little loser wants a best friend," and "Loser!" and "Pa-the-tic!"

Mirta slumped in her seat and began to doodle once more. She was beginning to have serious doubts as to whether she would ever fit in at Cloud Tower.

Chapter 12

At Red Fountain, Riven peeked around the corner and into Brandon and Sky's dorm room. He was after any information he could get. The info wasn't for him though. It was for someone else, a very special girl. With Riven's good looks and mysterious demeanor, he could easily date many of the girls at Alfea. His spiked, purple hair set him apart from most of the other boys. However, he didn't want to date a fairy. He wanted a witch. And not just any witch — he liked Darcy. That was who he spied for as he peered through the open doorway.

Timmy sat on the floor next to several blueprints. He adjusted his glasses and pointed to something on the paper. "Cloud Tower is surrounded by a magical protective field, Brandon."

Brandon knelt beside Timmy for a closer look. "Okay, is there any way to get through it?"

Timmy ran his finger along a winding representation

of a corridor. "I think I could map out a path so you could get in."

"Awesome," said Brandon. "So I could go in tonight, right?"

Riven heard a bed creek and Sky entered his limited view. "You might not want to go tonight, it's a full moon," Sky warned. "Witches are particularly strong during a full moon. Their powers can sometimes double in strength."

"I know," said Brandon. "But Bloom was seriously upset today. She needs this."

"All right." Sky crossed his arms. "Just be extra careful. It's risky."

"Hey. How fast can your levabike fly?" asked Timmy.

Riven silently inched his way away from the open door. When he was clear, he turned and strode down the hallway. "Brilliant," he said with a smile. "I have to report this!"

Riven ducked into an empty supply closet. He placed his fingers on his temples and concentrated on Darcy.

Puppy Dog to Stiletto, he projected. *Come in, Stiletto.*

Suddenly his thoughts were filled with two eyes — two wickedly beautiful eyes.

What do you have for me, Puppy Dog? asked Darcy.

Riven smiled. *The pixie is coming to Cloud Tower . . . tonight!*

In his mind, he sensed Darcy smiling also. *Well, we'll make sure to have a wonderful welcome waiting for her!*

CHAPTER 13

That night, as Bloom lay in bed, she replayed the test in her mind — for what seemed like the hundredth time. She analyzed every move, every leap, and every dodge. She thought of tons of different ways she could have beaten the obstacle course. The trouble was that she hadn't thought of any of those ways during the test itself. If only she were more confident in her powers.

Tap-tap-tap.

"Huh?" said Bloom. The noise sounded as if it came from the balcony door. She glanced over at Flora. Her roommate was still fast asleep in her own bed.

Bloom quickly threw on her sweats and opened the door. She timidly stepped out into the cool night air. "Uh . . . hello?"

Brandon rose into view. "Hey!"

"Hi!" Bloom leaned over the railing and saw that he sat on his red levabike. His helmet was tucked under one arm and his blond hair danced in the breeze.

"I hope you don't have any big plans for tonight," he said.

A bit surprised, Bloom laughed nervously. "Oh, I don't know. Would counting sheep be a big plan?"

"Are you kidding?" Brandon laughed. He reached back and pulled another helmet off the seat behind him. He held it out for Bloom. "Hop on!"

"Where are we going?" Bloom asked as she took the helmet.

"Cloud Tower," he replied. "You wanted to get into the Book Chamber, so Timmy and I figured out how to sneak inside."

Bloom ran inside and quickly got dressed. She emerged again, then quietly closed the balcony doors. Then she climbed onto the back of Brandon's levabike. It was just like riding a motorcycle except it had no wheels and could fly.

Bloom strapped on her helmet and Brandon did the same. "While the witches sleep," he said, "we can get a look at your book."

Bloom smiled and wrapped her arms around Brandon's waist. She held on tight as the levabike pulled away and zoomed toward Cloud Tower.

CHAPTER 14

"I don't see what the big deal is," said Mirta.

Her roommate, Lucy, sat on her bed and shook her head. As usual, most of her long black hair hid the permanent scowl she kept on her face. "Hello!" Lucy said mockingly. "You stood there in front of the whole class and talked about some sappy friendship spell!"

"But, Lucy . . ." Mirta began.

"Look, Mirta," said her roommate, "we can't hang out anymore."

"So you'll hang with your new friends, Icy, Darcy, and Stormy?" Mirta asked. She pointed a finger at the gloomy girl. "Let me tell you something, those witches are not your friends. They don't even like you. All they want you for is to do their homework. They're just using you!"

Lucy didn't move or show any emotion. She simply sat there and stared at Mirta through her greasy hair. "Say what you want," she said. "The fact is that I can't be seen with a loser like you! What they say is true. You don't belong here."

"They?" asked Mirta. "Who are *they?*"

Lucy ignored the question. "Listen, in the future, if you pass me in the halls don't bother to say hello."

Mirta's vision blurred as her eyes filled with tears. She ran from her dorm room, down the hall, and toward the stairs. She didn't want Lucy to see her cry. She didn't want anyone to see her. Mirta sprinted up the stairs and emerged on the roof of her dormitory — one of the largest structures of the black castle that was Cloud Tower.

Mirta stomped over to the parapet and leaned over the edge. The night wind chilled her as she peered into the darkness below. As her eyes adjusted to the moonlight, she was able to make out foothills and forest below. An idea occurred to her.

She stormed to the center of the roof. "I'll show you, Lucy," she said. "I'll show you I was right." She raised her hands above her head. "I'll use an eavesdropping spell from the Holmsian Realm." Her hands began to glow. "I'll show you what Icy, Darcy, and Stormy really think about you."

Mirta closed her eyes and concentrated on the three witches. "*Search high and low, both cranny and nook,*" she chanted. "*When you find that witch, let me listen and look!*"

A blue tendril of smoke danced in front of her. Then it split and widened to create a border around and image of Icy, Darcy, and Stormy. The three witches were huddled in the Cloud Tower's Book Chamber.

"So this time, we'll steal Bloom's power," said Icy with an evil sneer. The young, ashen-haired witch held out her hands. Stormy entered Mirta's vision. Her wide, frizzy hair obstructed Mirta's view as she handed something to Icy. Stormy stepped away and Mirta saw that Icy held a large book. "When she reads the book," Icy continued, "she'll panic and be filled with doubt."

Darcy stepped into view. Her long brown hair framed a pretty face with a wicked smile and an evil sparkle in her eyes. "Her defenses will drop," said Darcy. "Then we'll rip the power right out of her!"

The three witches laughed as the vision slowly vaporized. When it vanished, so did Mirta's thoughts of Lucy. Now she worried about the fairy named Bloom. She had seen Bloom around and everyone had heard of the witches' dislike for her. Mirta knew that witches weren't supposed to like fairies. But Bloom didn't deserve to have her power stolen by those evil seniors.

"I have to stop them," Mirta said to herself.

CHAPTER 15

"**It's right up** ahead," said Brandon. "Hang on."

Bloom squeezed tighter as Brandon steered the leva-bike down toward a large lake. The bike evened out and flew a few feet above the water's surface. Huge wakes sprouted behind them as they raced across the lake and toward the forest beyond. After that, the ominous black spires of Cloud Tower came into view.

The Cloud Tower School for Witches was not just one tower. It was a giant castle made of several towers. The black spires jutted out and overlapped one another in a twisted yet elegant fashion. They each rose up to pierce the foreboding storm clouds that always seemed to hover above the school. The castle stood atop a gloomy mountain, surrounded by the Dark Forest. It was probably the most dreadful-looking structure in all of Magix.

Once Bloom and Brandon crossed the lake and neared the tree line, Brandon easily maneuvered the levabike over the treetops. In no time, the forest was behind them and the levabike rose to circle the school itself.

"We have to find the point of vulnerability of the force field," Brandon shouted. "It's the only way to get through it."

Bloom squeezed tighter as the levabike banked sharply. Currents of electricity cascaded over the dark spires as Brandon searched for their point of entry.

"It should be right below the place that has the highest voltage," said Brandon. He pointed to an unusually large bolt of electricity erupting from the central tower.

"Watch out!" yelled Bloom.

Brandon turned just in time as a bolt of lightning lashed out from above. The jagged beam struck the tower and seemed to feed the rest of the dancing currents. They all brightened at once. That was when Bloom saw the dark area between the two largest towers. That had to be the weak spot.

"That was close," said Brandon.

"I know where to go," Bloom announced. "Fly between those two towers!"

"You got it!" Brandon said as he pushed the levabike into one more dive. "Hold tight!"

As they sped downward, none of the cascading electricity moved toward them. Giant bolts of artificial lightning flashed all around them, but never at them. Only a few tiny tentacles of light reached their way. And they didn't seem to do any harm.

"It's working!" said Bloom.

She spoke too soon. One of the small energy beams zapped the front of the levabike.

"Oh, no, I'm losing power!" said Brandon.

Bloom noticed the levabike's steady vibration cease and felt them drop. Luckily, they were only a few feet from a large balcony. Brandon glided it down but they both tumbled off the levabike as it hit the surface and skidded sideways.

Brandon took off his helmet and dashed for Bloom. "Are you okay?"

Bloom stood and removed her own helmet. "Yeah," she replied. "Where are we?"

"Just where we need to be," Brandon answered. He reached into his jacket and pulled out an electronic pad. He pressed a button and the display screen came to life. A map of Cloud Tower appeared. Brandon pointed to an entry door at the other end of the large balcony. "The Book Chamber is that way."

"What is that thing?" asked Bloom.

"It's Timmy's latest invention," Brandon replied. They walked toward the doorway. "It's a witch tracker. It maps the movement of any witch within a hundred yards."

Brandon carefully opened the door. "Everyone's sleeping," he whispered. "As long as we're quiet, we'll be fine."

Bloom followed him as they descended a winding stairwell. She had been to Cloud Tower before. Now everything was coming back to her. They came to a dark door at the end of the stairs.

"This is it," said Bloom. "The Book Chamber."

They stepped inside a long and dark room. Dim candlelight revealed rows upon rows of bookshelves covering every wall. The books that weren't on the shelves were heaped in hundreds of tall stacks scattered around the chamber. Some stacks reached as high as the soaring ceiling. It was as if the magical chamber contained a special book for every living soul in Magix.

"How are you going to find your book?" asked Brandon.

"When I was here before, my book was already out," said Bloom. "Like it was waiting for me."

Brandon moved toward a book resting on a golden pedestal. An engraved image of Bloom was etched on its dusty cover.

"Hey, looks as if it's waiting for you again," said Brandon. He opened the thick book and thumbed through some of the pages. "You're only a freshman and look how big your book is! You must have a seriously awesome life story."

Brandon stepped aside as Bloom examined some of the cryptic pages. "I guess. I wish the only copy didn't have to be at Cloud Tower."

"Try asking it something," Brandon suggested.

Bloom knew that only more talented fairies or witches could actually make out the mysterious language written inside. However, anyone could ask the magical book a question. If they were lucky, the book would answer.

Bloom closed her eyes and placed both hands on the open pages. "Where do my powers come from?"

Immediately, Bloom's mind was filled with a vision of three ancient witches hovering in a void. One of the ugly crones flew closer. "You come from a long line of blood-thirsty witches," she announced. "The source of your power is the coven of darkness." She gave a shrill cackle and Bloom's vision changed. The witches disappeared and she saw a beautiful alien world suddenly fill with snow and freeze over. "You were created to spread misery throughout the universe," the witch continued. Bloom trembled as flames now filled her sight. Out of the flames floated the same red-haired baby she saw in her previous vision. It was Bloom as a baby. The witch's voice cackled louder. "This is the purpose for which you were born!"

Bloom couldn't take any more. She let go of the book and opened her eyes.

"Oh, no," she whispered. Tears ran down her cheeks.

"What's the matter?" asked Brandon. He placed a comforting hand on Bloom's arm. "What did it tell you?"

Bloom pulled away. "I don't think you want to hear it." She tried to wipe the tears from her face but more came. "It's too horrible."

"Whatever it is," said Brandon, "you can tell me."

"Okay," Bloom said in a trembling voice. "According to this book, I'm not really a fairy . . . I'm a witch." She hung her head.

"A witch?" Brandon took a step backward. "No way, it can't be. That's impossible!"

"I know," said Bloom. "I'm confused. What does this

mean?" She looked up and saw Brandon standing several feet away from her. His eyes were wide in disbelief. "Brandon?"

He didn't answer. He just hung his head.

"Listen," said Bloom. "If my powers are evil, I won't use them anymore." She turned away from him and cried harder.

Suddenly, she felt Brandon's hand on her arm. Part of her wanted to turn and be held by him — to hold him tightly and cry on his shoulder. But all she could see was that look of horror in his eyes.

"Just go, okay?" she said through clenched teeth. "I need to be alone. I need to think about this."

CHAPTER 16

The next morning, Stella hummed as she brushed her long blond hair. She pulled most of it back (except for a few strategically placed strands) and wrapped it with a thin blue ribbon. She took both ends of the ribbon and began to tie the special bow she always wore. If tied correctly, the bow mimicked the starburst pattern on her scepter. It was a constant reminder to everyone that she was the Princess of Solaria. She almost had it when a knock at the door made her slip and mess up the bow entirely.

"Who is it?" Stella barked.

"It's Flora," said a gentle voice from the other side.

"Ugh!" Stella untied the bow and quickly began to lash it back together as she stomped toward the door. "Haven't I told you? Eight to nine is always hair hour!"

"It's an emergency," said Flora.

Fumbling angrily, Stella quickly tied the bow and flung open the door. "What's the matter?"

Flora raced into Stella's bedroom. "Bloom never came back last night!"

Stella forgot all about her bow. "What?"

Tecna and Musa marched into the room. "We just talked to Brandon," said Tecna. "Bloom insisted on walking back."

"From Cloud Tower!" Musa added.

"All by herself?" asked Stella.

"She could be stuck in the Dark Forest," said Musa. "She could be lost!"

Stella ran to the door. "We have to find her before something awful happens!"

CHAPTER
17

Deep in the Dark Forest, something stirred beneath a pile of leaves. A hand erupted from its center. The leaves rustled some more, then Bloom sat up and yawned.

She looked around. "It's morning?" She pulled a few leaves from her hair. "I must've fallen asleep."

Bloom got to her feet and brushed herself off. The Dark Forest wasn't so dark in the daytime. Yet, she still had to be careful. Being this close to Cloud Tower, there was no telling what she might run into.

Bloom supposed walking back hadn't been the smartest thing to do. She just couldn't face Brandon knowing that she was a witch. She could tell it bothered him. She wondered what was going to happen to their relationship.

As Bloom started down the trail toward Alfea, she sensed something. Someone was watching her. Her suspicions were confirmed when she heard a light rustling behind her. She spun around and spotted a figure duck behind a tree.

"Hey!" Bloom yelled. "I can see you hiding back there!"

A young girl timidly stepped into the clearing. The hair was much shorter than Bloom's red locks. She wore a mix of different types of clothing — a black skirt over red stockings, a black vest over a torn white T-shirt showing a picture of a jack-o'-lantern, thick black bracelets, and black army boots.

"Hi, I'm Mirta," said the girl. "I've been trying to find you, Bloom."

"How do you know who I am?" asked Bloom.

"When Icy has someone in her sights," Mirta replied, "everyone knows." She ran up to Bloom. "And that's why I'm here. Icy, Darcy, and Stormy are after you. You're in a lot of danger!"

CHAPTER 18

Stella led the way as she, Flora, Tecna, and Musa ran through Alfea's main gate. They dashed across a clearing and stopped at the edge of the Dark Forest.

"Wait a minute," said Stella. "How are we going to find her?"

"Only one way," said Flora. "We're going to need everyone's powers!"

"Let's go, girls!" shouted Musa.

Each of them crossed their arms and began the transformations. Energy washed over them and their clothes magically morphed into their fairy outfits. Stella's fairy wings emerged as her clothes were exchanged with a golden two-piece. Flora was now dressed in a glittering pink dress shaped like petals from a flower. Musa danced in midair as she sprouted silky wings and wore a shiny red miniskirt and boots. Bright green energy crept over Tecna's body until she was dressed in a sparkling gray jumpsuit, complete with neon fairy wings. The four fairies hovered over the clearing like four beautiful hummingbirds.

"*Floral navigator!*" Flora cried. She waved her hands, and dozens of dazzling flowers leapt from her fingertips. They swirled like a tornado, then disappeared into the ground. For a moment, nothing happened. Then hundreds of golden flowers sprouted from the soil. They were arranged in the shape of an arrow pointing in Bloom's direction.

"Cool!" said Stella.

"All right," said Flora. "We need to go east." She dropped down and hovered with the others. "She is definitely in that direction."

Musa took to the sky above them. "I'll bounce some ultrasonic waves to probe the area!" She balled up her fists and squeezed her eyes shut. Suddenly, the air around them was filled with music. Driving drumbeats and whines of electric guitars penetrated the dense forest beyond. As the music began to fade, Musa opened her eyes and cocked her head, listening for returning echoes. "I have a reading!" she announced.

"Air-synch it over to me," Tecna instructed. "I'll analyze it."

Musa stretched an arm toward Tecna. A yellow burst of energy shot from her fingertips and into Tecna's awaiting hand. Tecna put her other hand to her head and closed her eyes. Her brow wrinkled as she concentrated.

Her eyes popped open. "I found her!" The others gathered close as Tecna held up an empty palm. An image of the forest appeared above her hand. The trees flowed through the image as if a flying camera had recorded the entire thing. The vegetation stopped moving and a yellow dot appeared among them. "Bloom is exactly . . . here," said Tecna as she pointed to the blinking light.

"Great work, everybody!" said Flora.

Stella flew forward. "Those things are very helpful," she said, "but we need the most important part." She soared above them with a spin. "I'm of course referring to what *I'll* contribute."

"What is it?" asked Tecna. "Don't keep us in suspense."

"But of course," Stella replied. "It's the Guiding Light!" She closed her eyes and concentrated. Soon, her entire body glowed like the beacon of a lighthouse. "I'll guide you to her exact location," Stella proclaimed. "Not to mention, I'll brighten up the Dark Forest!"

The others laughed as they joined her in the sky. They followed Stella as she dove toward the Dark Forest.

"The right kind of lighting can do wonders," said Stella. "Even for the most drab and dreary venues!"

Deeper in the forest, Mirta and Bloom sat in a large clearing. Mirta explained how she had used an eavesdropping spell to spy on Icy, Darcy, and Stormy. She told Bloom how they were planning to steal her power, yet again.

"So, you see," said Mirta, "the book was fake. You're not a witch after all!"

"Whoa," said Bloom. She sighed with relief. "I'm glad you told me. Thanks!"

Mirta smiled. "You're welcome!"

"But why did you?" Bloom asked. "Why are you so friendly? Aren't you supposed to hate me? I mean . . . you're a witch."

Mirta opened her mouth to reply, but was interrupted.

"As if," said a voice above them. "She's not a witch!"

Bloom and Mirta spun to see Icy, Darcy, and Stormy hovering above the treetops.

CHAPTER
19

"**Mirta is just** an annoying little wicca wannabe," Darcy said with a sneer.

"As well as a serious reject," Stormy added. "No one likes her. She's desperate for friends."

"So desperate, she'll hang out with a fairy!" Icy taunted. "Mirta, you're pathetic!"

Bloom leapt to her feet and glared at the three hovering witches. "Don't talk to her like that!"

Icy cackled. "Look, she's defending her. That is *so* cute." Her wicked smile transformed into a scowl. Her hands glowed bright white as she raised them above her head, ready to cast a spell. "And I despise cute!"

"*Illusion delusion,*" Mirta whispered.

"Hey, you!" boomed another voice.

Bloom and the witches turned to see Stella and the rest of the Winx Club. They stood defiantly on the other side of the clearing.

"Why don't you try and fight us?" Stella challenged.

Stormy sneered. "I'll get rid of them." With a flick of her wrist, a giant tornado appeared. It thundered toward the interfering fairies. They quickly leapt out of its path.

"Don't fall for that, Stormy," said Darcy. "It's just a first-year, freshman trick." She put two fingers to her temple. "An illusion that Mirta created."

Waves of energy flowed from Darcy's eyes. They washed over Stella and the others and made them blink out of existence.

Darcy smirked at Stormy. "Frankly, I can't believe you let a freshman trick you like that. So sad."

Stormy growled with frustration.

"Hey, firstie!" yelled Icy. "That might have been an illusion, but this isn't!" The witch thrust out her hands and blasted them with an intense beam of light. "*Ice coffin!*" she yelled.

ZAP!

Mirta hid behind Bloom as the blast hit them. Immediately, ice formed over the two girls. The freezing cold air paralyzed Bloom. She could still see and hear everything, but she couldn't move and she couldn't use her Winx.

"In a matter of minutes, Bloom will be so weak, she'll just hand us her power," Icy gloated. "It'll be ours and . . ." *BAM!* A flash of golden light slammed into Icy's back. She tumbled through the air.

"*Ice coffin,* oooh," Stella mocked. "How predictable."

Stella hovered above the trees with the rest of the Winx Club — the *real* Winx Club. "She needs to majorly update her attack collection!"

Stella turned to Bloom and Mirta. "*Sun power!*" Two golden shafts burst from her outstretched hands. They washed over Bloom and Mirta's frozen tomb. The ice quickly dripped away and they were free.

Icy held her head as she flew back to join the other witches. "You annoying fairy!" she bellowed. "I can't stand you! You are *so* over!"

"No, you're over!" Mirta shouted defiantly.

"Oh, please." Stormy sneered. "This isn't even a contest!" She flew toward the fairies. Raising both arms, Stormy made *two* tornadoes appear. The twirling cyclones criss-crossed toward the fluttering fairies.

"Stay together!" Musa cried.

"Good idea!" said Darcy. She flew to Stormy's side and cast her own spell. A long energy rope appeared and bound the fairies together.

Bloom watched as the twin tornadoes bore down on her friends. She couldn't take anymore. "Stop!" She crossed her arms and began her transformation. Fire rippled over her body, changing her into a fairy.

Her wings beat madly as she flew to save her friends. Unfortunately, she didn't see that Icy had gotten behind her. *SMACK!* A blast of frozen energy struck her from behind. She tumbled from the sky and crashed through the trees.

"Bloom!" yelled Mirta.

"They thought they were cool!" Icy laughed.

"They thought they were tough!" added Stormy.

"They're nothing," proclaimed Darcy.

Bloom pulled herself off the ground in time to see Mirta step forward and raise her arms. *"Illusion delusion!"* yelled the young girl.

Suddenly, a giant monster appeared just behind the three witches. The creature had slimy green skin and was as big as Cloud Tower itself. It bore giant fangs and glared at the witches with seven yellow eyes. It raised its talons and opened its tooth-filled mouth.

ROOOOOOOOOOOAAAAAAAAR!!!

Even though it was an obvious illusion, the witches were startled with fear. The two tornados began to flicker.

"I'm losing them!" shouted Stormy.

The energy ropes loosened and dropped from around the fairies.

"It broke my concentration!" yelled Darcy.

"She tricked you again!" sneered Icy. She turned to the young girl on the ground. "And you, Mirta," she said. "Everything about you is annoying me right now!" She floated closer.

"Leave her alone!" Bloom shouted.

Icy ignored her. The witch's attention was focused on Mirta. "Your stupid tricks, your good attitude, even your stupid little pumpkin T-shirt." Mirta backed away, but Icy descended swiftly. "If you like pumpkins so much, maybe you'd like to be one!"

Bloom stumbled to her feet. She finally caught her breath, but she was still dizzy. She watched helplessly as Icy clapped her hands together and created an intense ball of energy. She flung it at Mirta and struck the girl point-blank. *ZZZZZAP!* In the blink of an eye, Mirta was transformed into the pumpkin on her shirt.

"Nooooooo!!!!!" screamed Bloom.

The witches cackled at Icy's neat little trick. The more they laughed, the angrier Bloom became.

"I told you to leave her alone," Bloom said through clenched teeth. She could feel fire burning inside her.

The witches must have seen something in her eyes. They stopped laughing and their own eyes widened.

Bloom became consumed with fury. Her internal fire grew until she felt like she would explode. She glared at the three wicked witches while the pressure built inside her. They had begun to back away as Bloom growled with anger. Then, with every fiber of her being focused on the witches, Bloom released the pressure.

KA-VOOOOOOOOM!

CHAPTER 20

Once again, Bloom found herself buried in a pile of leaves. She heard her friends moaning nearby. They must have gotten caught in the explosion ... or spell ... or whatever Bloom had done. She didn't know what had happened.

"That was some major Winx!" said Stella.

"Bloom, your power rocks," said Musa. "Wait, where is Bloom?"

"Yeah, where is she?" asked Tecna.

"We lost her again?" asked Stella.

Bloom sat up. "Hello! I'm over here!" The rest of her friends sat in the clearing. Just like her, they were no longer dressed as fairies.

"Bloom!" they said in unison.

Bloom picked a leaf from her hair. "Thanks for coming to save me, guys."

"You really sent those witches flying," said Tecna.

Musa looked around. "Did anyone see where they went?"

"I hope I sent them to another dimension," Bloom chuckled.

Flora stood and walked over to the jack-o'-lantern. "Who's the pumpkin?" she asked.

"That's Mirta," replied Bloom. "She's a witch but she's cool."

Flora knelt beside the pumpkin and stroked one of its leaves. "It's going to be really hard to turn her back. That was a witch-on-witch spell."

"I guess we'd better take her back to our crib," suggested Musa.

"Or find a place to plant her!" Stella joked.

"Stella!" yelled Bloom.

Stella smiled. "Kidding. Just kidding."

That night, Bloom was ready for bed early. She climbed under the sheets and was drifting to sleep almost as soon as she pulled the blanket over her. Before she went under, she heard Flora enter the room. Bloom rolled over and watched as her roommate watered her plants before turning in.

"Nighty-night, Bloom," said Flora. "It's good to have you back safe and sound, sweetie."

"It's good to be back," Bloom said softly.

Flora glided to where the Mirta pumpkin sat. She gently stroked one of the large leaves. "Don't worry, Mirta," she whispered. "We'll find a counter spell for you soon. But in the meantime we'll take good care of you." Flora leaned over and gave the pumpkin a gentle kiss on what would have been Mirta's forehead. "Welcome to Alfea."

Bloom smiled and drifted to sleep.

CHAPTER 21

The next week went by fast. Bloom was so tied up in homework, incantations, and Miss Griselda's famous "pop" quiz that she hardly spoke to Brandon at all. She was able to call and tell him that she wasn't a witch after all, but something still wasn't right. He seemed to believe her, but he still acted strangely when they spoke on the phone.

The next weekend, Bloom helped Stella during her "hair hour." She dipped a small brush into a smelly, green paste and brushed it onto Stella's long, blond locks.

"How much time do you think you spend on your hair every day?" Bloom asked.

"Ask not what I do for my hair, *dawling*," Stella replied with a regal flick of the wrist. "Ask what my hair does for me!"

They both giggled as Bloom painted on another layer of green goop. "So what is this stuff anyway?" asked Bloom.

"It's Flora's own botanical-slash-magical formula," Stella

said proudly. "In three minutes my hair will shine like glass."

"That's cool," said Bloom. She loaded the brush with some more paste.

Stella stared behind her at Bloom through the mirror. "Is something wrong?"

"I'm just kind of bummed, I guess," Bloom replied.

"You have that look on your face," Stella said, turning and putting a hand to her chin. "It's Brandon, isn't it?"

"He said he would call and he never did," Bloom said. "And the Day of the Royals is tomorrow."

"He didn't invite you?"

"No."

"Fret not, my dear," Stella said with a wide grin. "The problem is quite easily solved. You simply have to coax the invite out of him."

"Coax it out? How do I do that?"

Stella picked up the phone. "You call him."

"But what am I supposed to say?" asked Bloom.

Stella held the phone out to Bloom. "First comment on something else, like the weather, then segue into dropping hints. Just be casual."

Bloom took the small phone. "I could try."

"Fab!" Stella exclaimed.

Bloom smiled and held the phone out to Stella. "Or I could just drop him a text."

Stella pushed the phone back to her. "Nope. He needs

to hear your lovely voice." She grabbed a towel and walked toward the bathroom.

"Where are you going?" asked Bloom. "I need emotional support!"

Stella waved her off. "Don't worry, you'll be dandy. I just have to triple wash my hair." She disappeared through the doorway.

"I can wait," Bloom called after her.

"Nah-ah. Call him!" Stella shouted.

Bloom got up and went to her room. She plopped down on the bed and dialed Brandon's number. "Just sound casual," she said as the phone rang.

"Hello?" said a voice at the other end.

"Hey!" Bloom chirped. "How about this weather?"

There was a short pause. "Hey, is that you, Bloom?" asked Brandon.

Bloom cringed. She must have sounded so stupid. "It's me!" she said, trying to sound casual but knowing she was failing miserably. "Have you happened to notice how nice the weather has been the past few days?"

There was another confused pause. "It's nice."

Bloom bit her lower lip. "If you think today's nice, wait until tomorrow. I hear it will be clear and sunny all day long."

"That's good to know," said Brandon. *He* certainly had the casual thing down.

"Oh, yeah," said Bloom. "It promises to be a nice little day. It'll be perfect for that thing you guys are doing tomorrow. What was that again?"

"Just . . . the Day of the Royals," replied Brandon in a quiet tone.

"Right," said Bloom. "It should be a fun day. I've never been . . ."

"Beep!" said Brandon.

Did Brandon just say, 'beep'? "What was that?" asked Bloom.

"Uh . . . that's my call waiting!" he said nervously. "I should probably get that. Beep! I'll talk to you later!"

Click.

Bloom stared at the phone. "That was so lame."

Stella entered the room, drying her hair with a towel. "So, when is he picking you up?"

"He beeped me, Stella."

"He beeped you?" Stella threw the towel over her shoulder and snatched the phone from Bloom. "I'll call Sky and straighten this out. I'm sure Brandon didn't mean to diss you like that!"

Bloom put her hand over the phone, stopping Stella from dialing. "I don't know, Stella."

CHAPTER 22

"I feel terrible," said Brandon. He paced back and forth in Timmy's dorm room. "Bloom just called me and I was totally cold." He sat on the bed and ran a hand through his hair. "I don't know how I'm going to pull off this weekend."

Timmy slapped him on the back. "Hey, it'll be fine."

Brandon turned to him with wide eyes. "Diaspro's coming."

"She is?" Timmy asked. "Uh-oh."

"Yeah," Brandon sighed. "But all I can think about is Bloom. I need help."

Timmy got to his feet. "All right, there must be a logical solution." Now it was his turn to pace across the room. "A rational approach . . ." he said, then snapped his fingers. "I've got it!"

"What?" asked Brandon.

Timmy leaned forward and adjusted his glasses. "Get out of town as fast as you can!"

"Come on, dude," said Brandon.

Timmy gave him a dismissive wave. "Tomorrow, just keep a low profile and keep your helmet on! Now go call Bloom and apologize."

Brandon got to his feet. "Yeah. I'll call her right now. I'll tell her how I really . . ." He almost slammed into Riven.

"You're so pathetic," said the spike-haired boy. "You're getting all worked up over a girl like Bloom!"

"What?" asked Brandon. He couldn't believe it. Riven had never been too fond of Bloom and her friends. But he'd never come out and said anything before.

"Why do you even want to be seen with that little pixie?" Riven asked. "It's common knowledge that she tried to go out with every guy at Red Fountain."

"Shut up, Riven!" yelled Brandon. He punched him in the stomach as hard as he could. He wasn't going to let Riven get away with saying those things about Bloom.

Riven doubled over and gasped for air. Brandon felt some of his anger subside. Riven always said stupid things. Had he deserved what Brandon gave him? Was Brandon that angry with him? Or was Brandon really angry with himself for the way he had treated Bloom?

He was about to help Riven up when the boy bent sideways and landed a kick square into Brandon's chest. He went flying down the hall and tumbled to a stop on the floor. Riven was on him, pounding him in the face as many times as he could. Brandon caught the last blow. He strained as he held Riven's fist in his hand. Then he kicked the boy off him and pinned him to the ground. Now it was Brandon's turn to pound Riven.

"Hey! Stop it!" Sky yelled. He grabbed Brandon's arm and pulled him off Riven. "That's enough! Break it up!" The two fighters faced off again but Sky stepped between them. He turned to Brandon. "Are you all right?" asked Sky.

"Yeah," said Brandon. He glared at Riven.

"How about you, Riven?" Sky asked. He put a hand on the boy's shoulder. "Are you all right?"

Riven didn't answer. Instead, he grunted and slapped Sky's hand away.

"Hey!" shouted Sky. "You always have so much 'tude! What's your problem, Riven?"

"What's *your* problem?" Riven mimicked.

Sky balled his fists and stepped closer to Riven. "I hope I draw you in sword and shield combat tomorrow!"

"Bring it on," Riven growled. He leaned closer to Sky. "I'll wipe you out!"

Brandon thought an entirely new fight was about to begin.

"Gentlemen, gentlemen," said a voice behind them. Headmaster Saladin approached the group of boys. The short, gray-haired man stepped between Riven and Sky. "Tomorrow is an important day for all of us here," said Headmaster Saladin. "Sky's parents, the King and Queen of Eraklyon, will be here personally." With his hands behind his back, the older man turned slowly to look everyone in the eyes. "I expect only your best behavior."

"Yes sir!" said Timmy, Brandon, and Sky.

Headmaster Saladin turned to Riven. "Riven?"

"Yes sir," the boy answered.

The headmaster moved closer to the angry boy. "Decorum is essential tomorrow," he said. "Do not attempt to settle this in the field."

CHAPTER 23

Bloom, Stella, and Flora marched into Musa and Tecna's room. It was such a lively place filled with all the latest computer and music equipment. Tecna had no trouble at all as she worked on her five computers simultaneously. Musa had stacks and stacks of all the latest CD's. She also had all the latest stereo equipment with which to play them.

Both occupants had their backs to the door when the group walked in. Tecna worked at her computer station as usual. Musa played her magical flute. While ethereal notes danced through the room, her music book hovered in front of her.

"Tecna, we need a map of Red Fountain," said Flora.

Startled, Musa lost her concentration. The music book fell to the floor.

"Sorry," said Flora.

"Are you going to the Day of the Royals tomorrow?" asked Tecna.

"We're sneaking in," Stella announced.

"Sky didn't send an invite?" asked Musa.

Bloom plopped on Musa's bed. "Neither did Brandon."

"Sky's parents are going be there," said Flora.

"They're actually the guests of honor," Stella said snidely. Bloom could tell her feelings were hurt just as much for not being invited.

"It's really not nice," said Flora.

"You know I'm not sure about this, guys," said Bloom. "Maybe we should stay here tomorrow."

"Don't you want to go?" asked Stella.

"I guess so," Bloom answered.

"Then you can't let a little detail like an invitation get in your way!" Stella explained.

Bloom smiled. "Okay, I'll do it!"

"Yay!" Flora clapped her hands. "How neat. I guess we're all going!"

CHAPTER 24

The next morning, Bloom and the others stood outside the gate to Red Fountain. A long line of spectators waited to get in. The line was moving fast, but Bloom was very nervous. The rest of the guests were much better dressed than Bloom and her friends. Bloom supposed they should have worn more than just their regular clothes. Then again, they weren't guests. They were sneaking in.

When the five fairies got to the head of the line, a tall Red Fountain boy stopped them. He looked much older than Brandon. He must have been a senior.

"May I see your tickets, ladies?" he asked.

"Certainly," Bloom replied as she reached into her pocket. She pretended to search for the tickets while she and the other girls casually sidestepped around him. Bloom then pointed to the boy's feet. "Oh, hey there," she said. "Your shoelace is untied."

When the boy looked down, Stella darted down the walkway. "Run!" she yelled.

The rest of the girls took off with Bloom close behind them. She could hear the boy's heavy footsteps behind her. "Hey! Get back here! Stop!"

The girls darted past finely dressed spectators as they tried to outrun the boy. Bloom nearly tripped over a woman's long dress. She stumbled but quickly regained her footing. Unfortunately, she fell behind the rest of the group.

Stella and the others turned a corner of a large building. Bloom hurried to catch up with them. As she turned the corner, she saw one of the doors click shut. That's where her friends went. Unfortunately, the boy was close behind her. If she were to follow them, he would surely see where she went. She looked around for another way to ditch him.

She leapt down some stairs and darted through an archway. Up ahead, she saw Red Fountain's large coliseum. From the roar of the crowd and the hum of the levabikes, Bloom knew that's where she would find Brandon. She poured on the speed as she headed straight for the huge structure.

As she neared it, she spotted a small maintenance building. With a nice lead over her pursuer, she darted around the building. Now, out of the boy's sight, she dove for a large hedge on the other side. She tried to calm her heavy breathing as she awaited his approach.

She peaked through the branches and saw his feet run into view. "Where'd she go?" he asked. Then he took off in a different direction. When Bloom heard his footsteps fade away, she knew it was safe to come out.

Bloom jogged toward the coliseum and tried to open one of the access doors. It was locked. She tried another. Locked. The third one wasn't. She quietly slipped inside.

Bloom could hear the crowd above her now. She was in one of the many access corridors under the coliseum. She didn't know her way around, but she wasn't worried. She could just follow the sound of the cheering fans.

After turning a few corners, the roar grew louder. She could also make out the sounds of levabikes and clashing of energy swords. The Red Fountain boys must be in the middle of a joust. She picked up her pace a little. She couldn't wait to see Brandon in action. She knew he was going to be great!

Bloom turned the last corner and saw the entrance to the coliseum seats. She saw levabikes streak across the field below. As she suspected, one boy held a green energy lance and battled a boy with an energy sword.

Bloom was about to look for a seat when she heard footsteps behind her. She turned and saw an approaching royal family. A large man with a dark beard and jeweled crown escorted an elegant woman wearing a stunning dress. Two guards escorted them, and a girl Bloom's age followed closely behind. She had long, pale blond hair and wore an elegant gown as well.

Bloom stepped to the side of the corridor as they approached. *This must be Prince Sky's parents*, she thought.

Just then, an announcer from the coliseum confirmed her suspicions.

"Ladies and gentlemen," he said. "He is a graduate of Red Fountain and an award-winning author. She is a former model and a philanthropist to educational charities. Friends of Red Fountain, please welcome the King and Queen of Eraklyon!"

As the royal couple strolled by, Bloom studied their faces. They didn't resemble Prince Sky at all. Then again, some people don't have a strong family resemblance.

"That's funny, I didn't hear them announce me," said a voice to Bloom's left.

Bloom spun around and slammed straight into the young girl she had seen walking behind the royal couple. Both she and Bloom were knocked to the ground.

"You little squiretee!" the girl cried. "You ruined my entrance!"

The blond girl's purse lay on the ground. Several of its contents were strewn about. Included was a small, flat holoprojector. The device sprang to life, projecting an image of Brandon — Bloom's Brandon.

"Hey," Bloom shouted. "What are you doing with a hologram of Brandon?"

"Who do you think you are? Don't you dare question a royal princess!" ordered the girl. The two bodyguards rushed in to help her up. "I will have you fired faster than you can say 'sorry, Your Highness'!" The guards snatched up her purse and the rest of her belongings, including the hologram of Brandon. The rude girl didn't answer Bloom's question. "You are a disgrace to servants everywhere!" she yelled instead.

As Bloom sat there, staring in disbelief, the two men escorted the girl down the corridor. "What a total loser," barked the princess as she entered the coliseum.

Bloom slowly got to her feet. *Why would she have a picture of Brandon?* she thought. Then it all made sense. The pale blond hair, the sneering lips, the high and mighty attitude — that was no princess. That was Icy in disguise!

CHAPTER 25

That has to be it! Bloom thought. Icy was trying to sabotage the Day of the Royals! Or maybe it was something else. Maybe Icy had a spell on Brandon all along. Maybe that's why he had been so cold to her lately. Icy wanted to steal Brandon from Bloom to further torment her. Or perhaps it was a trap. Maybe she planned to use Brandon as bait in order to steal Bloom's power! Whatever Icy's plan, Bloom wasn't going to let her get away with it. Disguise or not, Bloom was going to take her down!

Bloom stepped through the doorway. Below she saw one of the helmeted Red Fountain boys fire magic missiles into the air. Another boy banked his levabike and threw out a handful of purple blades. They intercepted the missiles and exploded harmlessly above the field. The crowd roared with approval.

Bloom turned her attention away from the show and toward the problem at hand. She had to find Icy. She scanned the crowd until she saw a bright purple awning.

Beneath it sat the King and Queen of Eraklyon along with Icy in disguise. Their two escorts stood guard behind them. Bloom had to think of a way to draw Icy away from the guards as well as the spectators. After all, Bloom certainly didn't want to ruin the festivities.

She walked toward the royal group and tapped one of the guards on the shoulder. "I have a message for the princess," Bloom said in the sweetest tone she could muster. Then she whispered in his ear. The guard immediately leaned over and whispered something to the princess.

"The press wants to see me?" she asked.

Bloom snapped to attention. "I will escort you to the press box, Your Highness."

The girl rose and shuffled toward the aisle. "Please excuse me," she told the king. "I'm needed. *Teen Fairy* wants an interview with me." She adjusted her tiara. "I guess they want me to discuss my style secrets."

Bloom walked up the aisle. She was followed by the guard and the . . . *princess*. When they were in the corridor and out of the view of the spectators, Bloom raised a hand and snapped her fingers. "*Napus!*"

The guard collapsed behind her. A goofy smile stretched across his face as he slept.

"Hey! What do you think you're doing?" asked the girl.

Bloom spun around. "Oh come on, Icy! I am *so* on to your trick!"

The princess took a step back. "Oh, dear! Not another crazed fan!"

Bloom moved closer. "I don't know if you're trying to hurt Brandon or just ruin the Day of the Royals but I'm going to stop you!"

The princess tried to dart back to the coliseum seats. Bloom quickly dashed around her, cutting off her escape.

"Get out of my way, you crazy stalker!"

Bloom smiled. "That's not going to happen, *Icy*."

Bloom crossed her arms and closed her eyes. Fire flowed over her as she transformed. When her fairy wings appeared, Bloom pulled her hands back and summoned a searing ball of energy. The princess raised her own hands in defense but it was too late. Bloom hurled the sphere toward her foe. *BAM!* It slammed into her, sending her flying backwards. The girl zipped down the corridor and bashed through the opposite wall. *KRASH!*

CHAPTER 26

Stella led the way as she and the rest of the girls traveled through corridors under the coliseum. She hoped Bloom was having better luck finding Brandon than she was at finding Sky. In fact, they couldn't even find their way to the seats. The coliseum seemed to be honeycombed with endless passages and corridors.

They turned a corner and saw an approaching group of spectators. They tried to act casual as they passed by. Stella looked back at the ladies' elegant gowns and the men's handsome attire. She hadn't dressed up at all, which was very unusual for her. What a way to meet Sky's parents for the first time.

"Now I'm having outfit doubts," Stella admitted. She bit her lower lip. "I should have worn a dress!"

"It's a bit late to worry about that now," said Tecna.

Stella shook her head and smiled. "You're right. Anyway, it doesn't matter." She walked faster. "Parents love me.

It's the combination of my royal upbringing and signature bubbliness. It never fails me!"

"Of course Sky's parents will love you," said Musa. "Who wouldn't love an alliance between Eraklyon and Solaria?"

"True," Stella agreed. "I can see it now . . . our empire will be vast and powerful!"

"Hey, look," said Flora. "They're racing now!"

Stella glanced back to see Flora peering through a large crack in the wall. Everyone ran to join her.

Stella pushed closer. She saw several Red Fountain boys riding their levabikes around the huge coliseum. "Cute uniforms!" Unfortunately, they all wore helmets. Stella couldn't tell who was who. Then Musa pushed her out of the way. "Hey!" Stella yelled.

"Can you see Timmy?" said Musa.

Tecna playfully shoved Musa aside. "Okay, my turn!"

Stella pushed through the girls. "Okay, we're trying to find *my* boyfriend, remember?" She peeked through the crack once more. "And maybe I found him!"

Stella watched the levabikes zoom around the circular field. The boys still wore helmets so she didn't recognize any of them. However, two riders were in the lead. Stella was sure that one of them had to be Sky. He was very talented when it came to levabike racing.

Then Stella noticed one of the riders slow and fall behind the pack. He jerked his levabike to the right, making a tight u-turn. The boy poured on the speed as he flew around the track — in the opposite direction. When he neared the oncoming group of riders, he seemed to speed up a little. Then he brazenly plowed right between the two leaders. One of the riders slowed to a stop. The other boy lost control completely. His levabike twirled crazily and he was thrown free. He tumbled across the dusty field.

Stella gasped. "Oh, no!"

CHAPTER
27

Brandon stumbled to his feet. He removed his helmet and looked over at his levabike. It was a mess. He couldn't believe Riven had done that. Speak of the devil — Riven pulled to a stop next to Brandon.

"You're going down, Brandon!" yelled Riven.

"What were you doing, Riven?" asked Brandon.

"Just finishing what we started," Riven sneered.

"This isn't the time or place for this!" Brandon shouted. "You're going to make a scene!"

"I don't care," Riven said defiantly. He revved the engine on his levabike. "I'm going to take you out!"

Sky swerved his levabike to a stop between them. "Are you okay?" asked Sky.

"I'm fine," Brandon replied. "Riven's such a jerk."

Sky aimed his bike toward Riven. "Let's go and teach him a lesson!"

"Yeah, sure!" Riven laughed. "Bring it on!"

Suddenly, Timmy pulled up to the group. He took off

his helmet. "Hey, guys! Save it for later." He pointed to the large doors at the opposite end of the coliseum. "The dragons are coming out!"

The announcer's amplified voice boomed all around them. "And now, ladies and gentlemen! From lands different and unexplored, the Mustage dragons!"

The doors opened and the school dragons were released. First, their heads on long, serpentine necks poked through the opening. They scanned the audience with piercing, red eyes. Then the ground shook as they marched out on legs the size of large tree trunks. When they were in the open, they unfurled their long, powerful wings. Each dragon's wings were a different color — red, gold, blue, and green. One dragon snorted and two puffs of smoke shot from his nostrils. Two more dragons briefly sparred with each other, bashing their sharp black horns together.

"These wild and dangerous beasts are the fiercest dragons in all the known realms!" the announcer continued. "But fear not! Our sophomores have mastered the art of dragon wrangling. Using only their mind energy, they will control creatures once thought uncontrollable!"

Other boys ran onto the field and collected their leva-bikes and riders' helmets. Brandon, Sky, Timmy, and Riven faced off with the four dragons at the other end of the coliseum floor.

CHAPTER 28

Bloom flew after the retreating princess. They wound through the many corridors in and under the coliseum. Bloom cornered her in a large chamber with walls stretching to a high ceiling. The blond girl stood in the center of the chamber, fuming.

"I'm going to teach you a lesson in proper behavior," said the princess. She threw away her long cape. "*Quartz power!*"

Bloom watched as the girl transformed into a fairy. Her elegant gown faded to a short, red skirt. Sparkling red boots appeared on her feet and red jewels appeared on her fingers and on her tiara. Red wings sprouted from her back. Could Bloom be wrong in thinking this girl was really a witch in disguise? No way!

"That's a good imitation of a fairy, Icy," Bloom said. "But you're not fooling me!" *WHOOSH!* Bloom hurled another energy ball. The girl sidestepped and the blast hit the ground instead.

"You crazy wannabe!" yelled the princess. She charged straight for her. Bloom flew up, but the girl grabbed her by the ankle. She slammed Bloom back to the ground.

"You revolting witch!" Bloom snarled. She kicked the princess in the stomach, hurling her backwards.

The blond girl landed on her feet. "In spite of what the tabloids might say, let me assure you that I am not a witch!" She raised her hands into the air. A crimson ring formed over her head. "However, I can be witchy when needed."

She flung the ring toward Bloom. It slipped over her and shrank tightly. It bound Bloom's arms to her sides.

Bloom flew into the air. "Get this off me!" she yelled. She concentrated and strained against the ring. The fire burned inside her as she pushed harder. The ring gave a little then burst and disappeared.

Bloom snarled as she launched two fireballs toward the girl on the ground. The princess closed her eyes and a red shield appeared. *BAM-BAM!* The balls of fire burst as they slammed against the barrier. Then the princess flew up to Bloom in the air.

"What do you want?" she asked. "A lock of my hair, an autographed wing?"

"I will not let you hurt Brandon!" yelled Bloom.

The two girls faced off, hovering just below the tall ceiling, circling each other.

"*Crown jewel attack!*" shouted the princess.

Suddenly, six crimson jewels popped into existence around the girl. As she flew, the gems hovered in perfect formation around her. Then, one by one, red energy beams erupted from the jewels.

ZAP-ZAP-ZAP-ZAP-ZAP-ZAP!

Bloom's wings fluttered madly as she dodged the incoming blasts. Holes erupted in the wall behind her as she darted along.

"You're finished," Bloom said through clenched teeth.

She kicked off the wall and hurled another fireball toward the princess. *WHOOSH!* It hit her in the stomach and slammed her against the opposite wall.

The princess growled with frustration. "You're the one who's finished!"

CHAPTER 29

"**Our students are** demonstrating a dragon wrangling technique invented here at Red Fountain two centuries ago," said the announcer. "A highly focused form of telepathic projection."

Brandon held out a steady hand as he concentrated on his dragon. With their backs to one another, he, Sky, Timmy, and Riven stood in the center of the giant coliseum. Each one of them controlled one of the four large dragons. The boys were well-trained in dragon wrangling. So far, the demonstration was going off without a hitch. The four winged beasts peacefully flew in a circle around the boys.

"I'm taking you down, Brandon," Riven whispered. "You're history."

Brandon tried to ignore him. Maybe Riven was trying to get him to blow his concentration. If his blue-winged dragon flew out of formation, it would be quite embarrassing.

"I'm going to finish you in front of this whole crowd," Riven taunted. "My dragon is going to pulverize you and there's nothing you can do about it. As soon as I give him the signal, he's going to swoop in and you'll be humiliated in front of all these people."

Brandon wondered if his threats were real. Would Riven really disrupt the Day of the Royals for simple payback? Brandon didn't want to take any chances. Still concentrating on his dragon, he reached behind his back with his free hand. He removed an energy boomerang from his belt. With a flick of his wrist, he tossed it into the air. The tiny weapon flew high, arced, and then zipped toward Riven.

"Huh?" said Riven as he noticed the flying object. He jumped out of the way just as it flew straight for him. With his concentration broken, Riven's red-winged dragon broke formation and sat on the ground.

"You mean humiliated like that?" Brandon laughed. "I don't think so, buddy."

Riven got to his feet. "Bad move, *buddy*." He gestured toward the dragon and closed his eyes. Immediately, the red-winged dragon leapt to its feet and lunged for Brandon's blue-winged dragon. The two beasts roared and snarled as they began to battle.

"What are you doing, Riven?" asked Brandon. "They're going to get out of control!"

Riven only laughed. With a flick of his wrist, he commanded his dragon to fight harder. Many of the spectators began to scream and run from the coliseum. The beasts' battle intensified. Luckily, Timmy and Sky commanded their dragons to sit away from the intense combat.

"This is dangerous," Brandon scolded. "Rein in your dragon right now. Or I'll do it for you!"

Brandon extended both hands. He concentrated on his dragon, ordering it to fight back. The blue-winged creature swept its tail against its opponent. Riven's dragon was sent tumbling across the coliseum floor.

Riven growled with anger. "Now you're going to get it!"

He commanded his dragon to rise and take to the skies. The huge beast flapped its wings and rose from the ground. Brandon ordered his dragon to follow and attack. Riven's dragon turned in midair and rammed the blue-winged animal. Brandon's dragon dropped to the floor in a giant heap.

"Hey, man, calm down!" said Brandon.

"No way," Riven sneered. "I'm going to kick your dragon's butt and then I'm going to kick yours!" said Riven.

As Riven's beast dove for the final blow, Brandon saw Professor Codatora leap into the ring. The stocky, bearded man jumped onto Timmy's dragon and rode it toward the others. As he approached, the professor extended a long energy whip. A master dragon wrangler, Professor Codatora cracked his whip and yelled at the winged creatures. "Back in your pens!" he cried. The professor's dragon galloped between the two battling beasts. "Yah! Yah!" The loud whip startled the dragons into submission. Before long, he had all four dragons moving back toward the giant double doors.

Suddenly, the ground cracked in the center of the coliseum floor. Gold and red light flashed through the widening fissure. Everyone stepped away just in time. The ground exploded in a brilliant flash.

Brandon couldn't believe what he saw next.

Chapter 30

Bloom squinted as bright sunlight poured through the crack in the ceiling. She shut her eyes completely as dirt tumbled down as well. Luckily, she opened them just in time to dodge another barrage of crimson blasts from the gems surrounding the princess. Bloom was about to return fire but the girl swooped up and out of the crack. Bloom followed and soon found herself in the center of the Red Fountain coliseum.

"Who goes there?" asked a man riding a dragon. "Who dares disturb the Day of the Royals?"

"Bloom?" asked Brandon.

Bloom hovered above them, extremely embarrassed. Then several more red blasts of energy shot her way. She somersaulted in midair and formed a golden power shield around herself. The magical blasts bounced right off. Icy was still in disguise and still attacking.

"You're finished, witch!" Bloom shouted. She formed a ball of fire in each hand. "Stay away from Brandon!"

"Brandon?" asked the girl. "You mean that little squire boy? He's all yours!"

Bloom growled as she flung the fireballs at the girl's ring of gems. *KRACK! KRASH! KRUNCH!* One by one, they shattered around her. Bloom was relentless until all of them were gone.

"No!" cried the princess. "My crown jewels!"

Bloom formed one more fireball and hurled it toward her enemy. It slammed into her, knocking her from the sky. Helpless, the girl tumbled to the ground.

"Gotcha!" Bloom shouted.

"Diaspro!" Brandon ran to the fallen girl.

"Diaspro?" Bloom asked. She drifted downward. "You know her?"

The girl got to her feet and threw her arms around Brandon. "Oh, Sky!" she cried.

"Brandon?" asked Bloom. "What's going on?"

Diaspro glowered at her. "You worthless fan, his name isn't Brandon!" she shouted. "This is Sky, Prince of Eraklyon, and my beloved fiancé!"

Brandon pushed past the princess. "Bloom. Let me explain . . ."

Bloom floated down and sat on the ground. "You don't have to explain anything," she said. She felt tears filling her eyes.

Back in the corridor, Stella and the others crowded and pushed in around the crack in the wall.

"What's going on?" asked Tecna.

"Move!" shouted Musa.

"Come on," said Flora. "Let me see!"

"Hey!" said Tecna. "Don't push!"

Stella shoved her way in front of the crack and turned to the others. "Enough already!" she shouted. "It's my turn!"

Stella peered through the gap and onto the coliseum field. She watched the final battle between Bloom and some girl Brandon called Diaspro. Then that same girl called Brandon, Prince Sky. *What's up with that?* she thought. If Brandon was really Prince Sky, then who was the Sky she knew?

The King of Eraklyon rose from his seat. "Squire!" he bellowed. "Over here, now!"

Stella couldn't believe her eyes. She watched as Sky, *her* Sky, ran toward the king and knelt before him. "My Lord!" he said.

"Squire?!!" Stella yelled.

"Where's the security?" asked the king. "We pay your tuition at Red Fountain so you can protect our son!"

As the king continued to berate Sky, or whatever his name was, Stella just stood there in shock. All this time, she thought she was dating Sky, Crown Prince of Eraklyon. She had really been seeing nothing more than a measly squire. Stella would have felt utterly humiliated if she weren't so furious. Sky had lied to her. He had lied to Stella, and Brandon had lied to Bloom. Stella's anger grew as she watched her friend sit there on the field, crying.

CHAPTER 31

"**You left the** school grounds without permission," scolded Headmistress Faragonda. "You used your powers irresponsibly, and ruined the Day of the Royals!"

Bloom had never seen Miss Faragonda this angry before. The woman continued to chew them out while she paced around her office. Miss Griselda stood out of the way and simply glared at them with her usual disapproving eyes. Bloom and the other girls didn't say a word. They just stood there with their heads down and took their medicine.

"You sullied our reputation in front of the most important figures in Magix!" Miss Faragonda continued. She plopped into the chair behind her desk. She spun it around and looked out the window. It was as if she were too disgusted to even look at them.

"This is grounds for expulsion," Miss Griselda added.

After an awkward silence, Miss Faragonda spun back to face them. "She's right, you know," she said, peering over the rims of her glasses. Her voice had calmed somewhat.

"We'll have to meet with the council to decide whether you will be expelled or even invited back to Alfea next year."

"It's all my fault," Bloom muttered.

"Normally, we'd suspend your powers," said Miss Griselda. She turned to the headmistress. "But at this point in the semester I suggest dilution so they may continue their studies."

Headmistress Faragonda sighed. "That's fine."

"A fifty percent dilution should keep them out of trouble," said Miss Griselda.

Stella pushed forward. "But we told you how the boys lied to us!"

Miss Faragonda stood and looked angrier than ever. "That's no excuse," she countered. "You have abused your privileges and disregarded your responsibilities. You have disgraced Alfea!"

No one else said a word.

The girls didn't say much of anything as they returned to their dorm rooms. As they passed other students in the halls, they gawked at them with knowing stares. Word had spread quickly about the five girls who had their powers diluted.

Everyone turned in early that night. There was no chattering about boys, school, or clothes. The events of the day seemed to have taken all the fun out of them.

Bloom lay in bed, unable to sleep. She felt immense guilt for getting everyone punished. After all, she was the one who disrupted the Day of the Royals, not her friends.

If it weren't for her, they would still have all their powers. Bloom felt more out of place than ever.

Bloom waited until she heard slow, steady breathing coming from Flora's bed. Once she was sure her roommate was asleep, Bloom quietly got up and dressed. She carefully pulled her suitcase from her closet. As she began to pack her clothes, Kiko hopped onto the bed. The tiny bunny gave her a puzzled look.

"We're going home, Kiko," Bloom whispered.

Bloom finished packing and carefully opened her bedroom door. With the suitcase in one hand and Kiko in the other, she stepped out into the hallway.

"I got my friends in trouble, Kiko," Bloom said as she walked down the dormitory hallway. "I was made a fool of in front of the entire community. I'm the laughingstock of Magix." She jogged down the large stairway and opened the front door. "Brandon hasn't bothered to call," she added. "And his name isn't even Brandon. It's Prince Sky."

Bloom walked across the courtyard, toward the main gate. As she moved closer, the gate's giant fairy wing doors parted. Bloom stepped through then looked back at Alfea.

"I'm sure they'll understand if I don't say good-bye," Bloom said. She began to walk toward town. "Let's get out of here, Kiko."

Once in downtown Magix, Bloom made her way to the transport station. As she traveled, she gazed up at the wondrous buildings and structures. She also stared at the many places where she and her friends used to hang out. There was the fountain in the square, the coffee shop, and even the clothing stores where they used to shop. Bloom wondered if she would ever see any of this again.

Bloom was so busy taking in everything for the last time that she didn't notice something very important. She was being followed. A dark and familiar person in the shadows slowly kept pace with Bloom and her rabbit. The figure followed them all the way to the transport station.

"Welcome to the Magix Municipal Station," said a disembodied voice. "Please watch your step."

The station was no more than an open area between buildings. Very few people crowded the space. No trains, buses, or airplanes would stop there, either. It was a magic station.

"Where would you like to go?" the voice asked Bloom.

"Earth, please," she replied.

"Have a pleasant transport," the voice chirped.

The figure watched closely as Bloom was swallowed in bright light. When the brightness faded, Bloom was gone. The figure stepped out of the shadows and smiled.

"How interesting," said Stormy.

She ran back to the restaurant and found Icy and Darcy still sitting at their table. She quickly explained what she had seen.

"And she had this look on her face," Stormy continued. "She was all depressed."

Icy got to her feet. "Come on, girls," she said. "We're going to planet Earth!"

Darcy smiled. "What do we pack?"

"Just your toothbrush and your Whisperian Crystals," Icy explained.

"Without her fairy friends there to hold her hand, she'll be easy pickings," said Stormy.

Darcy beamed. "The Dragon Fire is finally going to be ours!"

CHAPTER 32

"I really messed up," said Bloom.

She slumped in the chair in her parents' living room. Her parents sat on the couch across from her. She waited for them to scold her or to send her straight back to Alfea, but neither of those things happened.

"Bloom, you're at a new school," her mother said with a kind tone. "With new friends, in a whole other dimension. Give yourself a break."

"Everybody makes mistakes," her father added. "It's part of growing up."

"That's right," her mother agreed.

"I still feel terrible about it," said Bloom.

Her mother strolled over and hugged her shoulders. "I know what you need," she said. "A couple days of your mom's home cooking. Tomorrow I'll make your favorite, pizza with extra cheese."

"I've done a lot of thinking lately," said Bloom. "Maybe I shouldn't even go back. I could stay here and go to a regular school." She placed a hand on her mother's arm. "You guys keep saying how happy you are that I'm at Alfea. Would you be disappointed in me if I dropped out?"

Her dad stood and joined Bloom and her mother. "We'll support you in whatever you choose," he said. "All we want is for you to be happy. That's what makes us happy."

Bloom was lucky to have such understanding parents. At that very moment, she felt as if she didn't ever want to go back. However, she knew that she should wait longer to make a final decision. She had a lot more to think about.

CHAPTER
33

"I can't let you go," the headmistress said sternly but serenely. "With your powers weakened, it would be far too dangerous. It's simply out of the question."

Stella couldn't believe what she was hearing. She and the others had stormed into Miss Faragonda's office, stood around her desk, and informed her that Bloom had disappeared. Granted, she had probably just gone back to Earth. But Bloom wasn't safe there. Stella knew more than any of them that things could be dangerous on that planet as well. All the while, the headmistress listened patiently to their proposal but quickly vetoed it.

"But we're worried about her," Flora pleaded.

"I understand," Miss Faragonda said in the same gentle tone. "Yet I cannot give you permission to leave the school grounds." She stood and crossed her arms. "Please allow me to remind you of your academic probation, young ladies."

"Bloom needs us!" Musa argued.

The headmistress pointed a finger at the opposite end

of the room. Her office door magically swung open. "This discussion is over," she said. "Go back to your classroom. You're dismissed."

Stella knew it was pointless to argue any further. She spun around and stormed out of the office. The others ran to catch up to her in the hallway. Stella continued to walk briskly but she was no longer frustrated. She had made a decision.

"I can't believe she said no," said Flora.

"Well," Stella began, "what does 'no' mean, really?" She kept walking and looking straight ahead.

Musa gasped. "What are you saying?"

"Don't answer that," said Tecna. "We're on probation. It's not a good time to take any risks."

Stella suddenly stopped and the others almost ran into her. She turned to face them. "Look, if I were missing, I'd want one of you to come looking for me."

"Word!" Musa agreed. "It's just so whack that we can't do anything about it."

"Sure we can," said Stella. A devious smile stretched across her face.

CHAPTER 34

The next afternoon, Bloom helped her mother in her new flower shop. Just as her mother predicted, she was able to build a bigger and grander store after the fire. Business was also better than ever. The shop was filled with customers. Bloom didn't know if her mother wanted her to go back to Alfea or not. But she could tell that her mom was grateful for Bloom's help that day.

Her mother stepped out of the storage room in the back of the store. She walked over to an older lady carrying several shopping bags. "I don't have any pink jigsaw blossoms left," she told the lady. "I'm sorry. We'll get some more tomorrow morning."

"What a shame," said the lady. "They're my daughter's favorite and today's her birthday."

Bloom turned her back to them and grabbed a pot of tulips from the shelf. After a quick glance to make sure no one was watching, she closed her eyes. She concentrated on the flowers in her hand. It took a bit longer with her diminished powers, but the spell came through. The tulips magically transformed into pink blossoms with petals shaped like pieces from a jigsaw puzzle.

Bloom turned toward her mother and the lady. "I found some," she announced.

The woman's face brightened. "Oh, thank you!"

After the woman paid and left, Bloom's mother eased up next to her. "Did you really find those flowers in the back?" she whispered.

Bloom smiled. "Flora taught me that trick." Then her smile faded. "I miss her."

Her mother hugged her. "Oh, cheer up, sweetie," she said. "We'll work everything out."

Once again, Bloom had no idea she was being watched. Across the street, Icy and the other witches stood just out of sight. Icy had witnessed that entire disgusting display of affection. It turned her stomach.

"No wonder she's such a big dork," Icy told the others.

Darcy placed her hands on her hips. "Like, can you believe this planet?"

Icy looked around the busy street. Boring, rectangular-shaped buildings lined the sidewalk. The people who walked in front of them were just as dull. All of them wore drab and dreary clothing. And *none* of them had magical powers.

"It's totally full of lamos," said Stormy.

"They shouldn't call it planet Earth." Icy chuckled. "They should call it planet Pathetic."

The others laughed at her brilliant joke. Then Icy looked back at her prey — poor, pathetic little Bloom. Soon she would have no magical powers at all. She'd finally be able to fit in somewhere. She'd fit right in with the rest of the powerless people on this pathetic planet.

CHAPTER 35

That night, after dinner, Bloom took Kiko for a walk around the neighborhood. She stroked his soft fur as she casually strolled beneath the streetlamps. Everything was quiet and peaceful. The only noises she heard were the sounds of an occasional passing car and a dog barking a few blocks away. There were no dragon roars, no explosions, and none of Musa's sonic booms. Bloom missed her friends terribly. Then again, maybe they were better off without her.

"Earth isn't so bad, Kiko," she said. "It's nice to be here again." She thought for a moment. "There's TV here, and tasty food, and of course, no witches. I could get used to the slower pace of things."

Bloom realized that she was only trying to convince herself to stay. Not only did she miss her friends, but everything else about Magix. She missed Alfea, the professors, and even Miss Griselda's pop quizzes.

There was something else she missed. It was a feeling.

The more Bloom thought about it, she realized that it was a feeling of belonging. On Earth, she was the only person with magical powers. In the land of Magix, almost everyone had them. She realized that she actually did belong there.

Bloom's powers were special, too. They weren't much since they were diluted, but she had some of the strongest powers her friends had ever seen. And where did she get those powers? Where did she come from in the first place? Bloom still didn't know who her birth parents were. She loved her adoptive parents more than anything, but she still had many unanswered questions about herself. One thing was for certain, she wasn't going to find any of those answers on Earth.

Then and there, Bloom decided she would return to Alfea. She would serve her sentence of diluted powers and be back to normal in no time. She would study hard, have fun with her friends, and try to put her past follies behind her — which definitely included Brandon. But most of all, Bloom would find out who she really was and where she came from.

Bloom practically sprinted back to her house. She couldn't wait to share her decision with her parents. They said they would support her no matter what she decided to do. Bloom hoped that she would make them proud and show them that she wasn't a quitter.

Once at her house, she leapt up the front steps and

threw open the door. Then Bloom couldn't believe what she saw.

"Get out of here, Bloom!" yelled her father. He was being held upside down by a huge, gnarled, thorn-covered vine.

Bloom's mother was held captive by Knut — a large, yellow-skinned ogre who worked for Icy, Darcy, and Stormy. And speak of the devils. The three witches stood in front of it all, cackling at Bloom's surprised reaction.

CHAPTER 36

"You!" Bloom yelled. "What are you doing here? What are you doing to my mom and dad?"

Icy stepped forward. "You have something that belongs to us. And we're here to collect!"

Darcy joined her. "We want your power, Bloom."

"And we're going to take it from you," Stormy added. She joined the others. "Unless, of course, you'd like to just hand it over."

"Never!" Bloom yelled.

"I was hoping you'd say that," said Icy. "This will be much more fun." She motioned toward the large ogre. He dropped Bloom's mother and took a step forward.

"It looks like you're going to have to deal with Knut," said Icy.

"He's new and improved because he's been working out," said Darcy. "You know, doing ogre pilates and such."

The giant beast charged forward. He did seem to be much faster. He ran forward and backhanded Bloom before she knew what hit her. She flew backwards and out the front door. She tumbled across the hard pavement outside. The ogre rushed after her, cracking the doorjamb as he pushed through the doorway.

Bloom stumbled to her feet. "I don't care if you're buff or not," she said. "It's Winx time!"

She crossed her arms and rose into the air. Fire burned inside her as she felt herself change into her true fairy self. The ogre jumped up and swiped at her feet but it was too late. Her transformation was complete. Her sparkling wings fluttered behind her as she soared higher. Then she thrust her hands in front of her. They glowed brightly as she drew power from within. *POW!* They exploded in a flash of light, flinging shafts of energy at the ogre. He flew backwards on impact, landing on the empty sidewalk.

Bloom's house seemed to ripple. As it did, the three witches passed through the solid front wall with ease. They looked down at the unconscious ogre with disgust.

"We are *so* not renewing his gym membership," said Icy. She turned her attention to Bloom. "As for you, fairy, you're over!"

The witches tried to surround Bloom. Instead, she flew back a few feet and circled to her left. That kept all the witches in front of her and in plain sight.

Icy floated forward. "Soften her up, Stormy."

"No problem," Stormy said. She flew up and pointed at Bloom with both hands. *KRACK!* Dazzling lightning exploded from her fingertips. Bloom dipped to her left just in time. The electricity shot past her and slammed into the side of her house. Chunks of brick littered her front yard.

Bloom had to get this battle away from there. With those three witches on the loose, there was no telling where fire, electricity, or energy balls would strike. She tucked her arms to her side and soared out of the neighborhood.

"Get her!" she heard Icy yell.

Bloom zipped through town, between the tall buildings of downtown and over the trees in the park. Once she was clear of most of the structures, she planned to turn and take the witches out once and for all.

Then something happened in front of her. The sky seemed to blur for a moment and then a giant net appeared. Bloom stopped as fast as she could before she slammed into the interlaced strands of energy.

"End of the line, pixie!" said Darcy.

Bloom spun around to see the witches right behind her. Bloom had flown as fast as she could. She wasn't expecting them to catch up with her so quickly.

"Like I always say," Icy sneered. "If it's got wings, pin it to the wall!"

The evil witch extended a glowing hand. Ice darts erupted from her open palm. The tiny shards flew toward Bloom at alarming speed. Without thinking, she concentrated as hard as she could. Immediately, a golden shield formed in front of her. The blades of ice shattered as they struck Bloom's protective barrier.

"She blocked you!" said Stormy.

Bloom was out of breath. She had done well against the witches so far. Yet she felt more drained than ever. At first, she didn't know why she was so tired. Then she remembered — her powers were diluted. It was taking everything she had to defend herself against these witches. She hoped her power was as strong as everyone made it out to be. She was going to need every last ounce to beat them this time.

"I'll take care of her," Stormy growled. She launched herself at Bloom, grabbing her by the throat. "Give us your power!" she roared.

"It's our destiny to have it!" Icy added.

"Never!" Bloom yelled. She desperately tried to remove Stormy's hands from around her neck.

Finally, the witch flung Bloom away from her as if she were a discarded spell book. Then she fired another lightning bolt. Bloom didn't have time to dodge it. Instead, she had to erect another energy shield. The effort drained her even further.

Stormy flew back to the others. "We're not breaking her," she said.

Icy crossed her arms. "Well, if she won't listen to us, maybe she'll be a good girl and listen to her mommy and daddy." Icy smiled and snapped her fingers. The three witches vanished.

"Oh, no," Bloom cried. She flew across town as fast as she could. "No, no, no!"

Chapter
37

Bloom was so tired, yet she pushed on. She darted past tall office buildings and under bridges. When she finally entered her neighborhood, she saw that her house's front door was open. She swooped inside and was terrified by what she saw.

"No!" yelled Bloom.

Bloom's mother and father were tied together and suspended in midair. A dark vortex swirled beneath them. All of the furniture in the living room had been sucked in. A small flowerpot was the last to go through. It sped across the room, circled the black hole once, then disappeared inside.

"Mom! Dad!" Bloom cried.

"You're just in time to see your parents disappear," said Icy.

"You better let them go," ordered Bloom. "Right this minute!"

"We're going to flush your parents right down the vortex toilet," said Stormy. "Unless we get your power."

"Don't do it, Bloom!" shouted her dad.

The fire in Bloom raged. "I'm warning you, Icy." She forgot how tired she was. "Let them go! This is between you and me!"

Icy turned to the others. "Flush them, Darcy!"

With a wave of her hand, Darcy sent her parents plummeting into the vortex.

"Noooo!" yelled Bloom. She flew in after them.

She dropped deeper and deeper into darkness. Up ahead, she saw a tiny little speck. It was her parents.

"Mom, Dad, hang on!" she yelled.

Bloom beat her wings as hard as she could. As she descended faster into the darkness, her parents grew closer. She tucked her arms to her sides and straightened her legs. She had to gain more speed. Darkness closed in around her, but she was almost there. She reached out for them. She pushed harder, flew faster, and her clawing hand grew closer.

Finally, she grabbed the rope binding her parents. With a secure grip, she turned and tried to fly in the opposite direction. For a moment, she seemed to be falling just as fast into the gathering darkness. She pushed harder, but still nothing. Then she reached deep inside herself, found some hidden reserve of power, and accessed it.

With tears in her eyes, Bloom began to slow their

descent. Slower and slower until they merely hovered in nothingness. Then she looked up at a tiny pinprick of light. She beat her wings harder and felt herself slowly rise. Tears flowed freely as the speck of light grew in size.

Her hand was numb, yet she kept a tight grip on her parents' ropes. Her arm felt as if it was being ripped from its socket, yet she kept flying upward. Higher and higher until she reached the swirling vortex. With one final push, she flew through, dragging her parents to safety.

"You look so tired," said Icy. "Why don't you have a seat?"

Bloom had barely gotten her bearings when a blast of ice slammed into her and her parents. Her mother and father were thrown safely away from the vortex. Bloom was sent sprawling into the dining room.

"You're up, Darcy!" Icy ordered.

Bloom began to rise when a blast of sonic energy struck her from behind. She flew end over end, slamming into the wall.

Stormy stepped forward. "My turn now!"

This time, they didn't even wait for her to get up.

"*Electric booty kick!*" yelled Stormy. Bolts of electricity erupted from her fingertips. They struck Bloom with full force, slamming her around the room.

"You've got no chance," said Icy. "Everyone knows your powers are diluted. It's been all over the chat rooms."

Bloom twitched on the floor. Was she awake? Was she alive? She could hear Icy talking but she could barely move. Her entire body ached and she felt as if she would pass out.

Instead, she reached forward and clawed at the carpet. Bloom tried, but she couldn't even get up to crawl.

"The Dragon Fire should be ours," Icy continued. "We've earned the right to have it." The witch strolled over to Bloom and knelt beside her. "Our coven spent centuries tracking its last remaining pieces. And when they finally located it on Sparks, they put a spell on the whole planet. They froze it, turning it into a sea of ice."

Bloom managed to push herself up. She used her last bit of strength just to sit up against the bookcase.

"The ultimate power was within their grasp," Icy continued. "But the Guardian of the Flame tricked them. That nymph hid the Dragon Fire inside the heir to the kingdom's throne." She poked a finger against Bloom's chest. "Inside you, Bloom."

That woke Bloom up a little. "You're saying that I'm the heir to the throne of Sparks?" she asked. "That I'm a princess?!"

"Yeah," Icy chuckled. "But once you lose the flame you'll just be a figurehead." She stood and walked toward the others. "All right! Let's finish what our coven started! Let's get the Dragon Fire!"

Using the shelves of the heavy bookshelf, Bloom pulled herself up. Once she stood on wobbly legs, she turned to face the witches.

"No," she said, trying to sound strong. "I won't let you take it."

Icy laughed at Bloom's last act of defiance. "It's *so* over for you." She reached out and sprayed Bloom with a plume of ice. "There's nothing you can do now."

Bloom was pushed back against the bookshelf. Her arms were pinned out to each side and ice covered her entire body. Only her head and shoulders were exposed. Bloom barely had the strength to move before she was pinned. Now she could do nothing at all.

"This is the part where the little freshman realizes she's been beaten," said Darcy.

"In a way, you're lucky, Bloom," Icy said as she stepped closer. She placed her cold fingertips under Bloom's chin and tilted up her head. "You'll be safe here on Earth while we use the Dragon Fire to summon the Army of Decay. Trust me, you do *not* want to meet them."

Icy dropped Bloom's head and joined the others. "Are you ready?" she asked. "Let's conjure the Whisperian Crystals!"

Bloom watched through blurred vision as the three witches formed a triangle in front of her. She tried once more to escape but it was no use. She was too weak.

"*Crystals of Whisperia,*" chanted the witches, "*dark magic from our kin, reach inside this girl and steal her power from within!*"

Three elegant crystals formed above their heads. Crimson electricity flowed through them, forming a floating, spinning triangle. As the triangle spun faster, Bloom felt something stir inside her. It was the fire she felt in battle, the fire she felt when she transformed. Only now, it didn't grow brighter, hotter. It shrunk and grew cold. Bloom tried to fight, tried to control it somehow, but she didn't know how. In the end, it continued to grow cold inside of her. It felt as cold as the ice that encased her.

Suddenly, she felt a pulling. Then a magical flame burst from her chest. Such a tiny thing, it hovered in front of her for a moment. It flashed once, then shot toward the spinning triangle. The crystals glowed with golden flames.

Bloom's eyelids grew heavy. Her head bobbed as she tried to stay awake. It was no use. She slowly slipped into unconsciousness. The last thing she saw was a golden glow transfer from the crystals to the three witches. The last thing she heard was their laughter.

CHAPTER 38

Bloom, said a woman's voice.

What a wonderful voice, Bloom thought as she floated.

Bloom.

I wish I could see her. Bloom looked around, but there was only darkness. *She sounds so beautiful.*

Bloom.

"Bloom?" said another voice. "Bloom, wake up."

Bloom slowly opened her eyes. Her father and mother knelt beside her. She slowly looked around. She noticed the disrupted house and remembered what had happened. She sat on the floor against the bookcase. What was left of her ice prison was melting and dripping behind her. Bloom was dressed in her regular clothes and she felt very cold inside.

"Are you okay?" asked her mother.

"I think so," Bloom replied. She slowly got to her feet. Her body was sore all over and she was extremely tired. Other than that, she felt uninjured.

"Are they gone?" Bloom asked.

"For quite some time now," her dad replied.

Bloom looked down and began to cry. *Everything* came back to her now. They had stolen her power. They had ripped it from her and left her empty inside.

Her mother hugged her close. "It's okay, sweetie."

Suddenly, bright light filled the room. A portal was being opened from the land of Magix.

"Oh no, they're back!" Bloom cried. She didn't know how much more she could take.

"Try to remain calm," her dad advised.

The portal grew brighter and larger. Then a dark silhouette came into view. *Which one is it?* Bloom thought. *Icy? Darcy? Stormy?* What would she do now? She had no way of defending herself or her parents.

The light faded until only the figure remained. It wasn't any of the witches.

"Stella!" yelled Bloom.

Her best friend ran to her and hugged her. "Bloom! Are you okay?"

"Not really," Bloom replied.

She explained how the witches followed her to Gardenia. She recounted how they threatened her parents and how she fought them to the end.

"The witches trapped me and took my power," said Bloom. "According to them, it's actually the Dragon Fire."

"Wow," said Stella. "That explains why you were able to

fight so well with your Winx diluted to half power." Stella turned to her parents. "I've heard legends about the planet Sparks and the Dragon Fire."

"They said that with it, they'll have unlimited power and be able to take over the whole universe," added Bloom's mother.

"What have I done?" Bloom asked.

Stella grabbed her by the shoulders. "You know what, Bloom?" she asked. "There is no way we are going to let them get away with this travesty. Nope. Nah-ah!"

"But what can we do?" Bloom asked.

"I say you and I hop the transportus back to school," replied Stella. "We find the other girls and get your power back."

"If anyone can do it," said her dad, "you can, honey."

Bloom gave a small smile. "Thanks!"

"I'll even pack you a slice of pizza for the road," said her mother.

Bloom threw her arms around her parents' shoulders. "You guys are the best!"

Tears flowed from Bloom's eyes as she realized just how lucky she was. With or without her powers, she had wonderfully supportive parents and loyal friends. She had been wrong to leave her friends at Alfea in the first place. She had also been wrong about fitting in. She was the last Princess of Sparks, after all. She belonged at Alfea and she belonged with her friends.

Bloom didn't know how, but she was going to get her powers back. She would do whatever it took. She also knew that her friends would be there to help her all the way. After all, they were the Winx Club!

Circle of Power

Winx CLUB ™

Magical Fairy GAME!

Find the Fairy Within You!

When You Play the Game
of
Magic and Friends

Winx Club Collectible Game Cards
Coming Spring 2005

Collect Them All!
Sun Rings
Scented Power Cards
Glitter Magix Cards

Check Out
the Fabulous
Fashion-Filled Pages
in the Debut Issue of
Winx Comic
Magazine
Spring 2005

UPPER DECK
ENTERTAINMENT™

www.winxclubgame.com

RAINBOW

© 2005 The Upper Deck Company.   Winx Club™ © 2005 Rainbow S.r.l.